Frozen Summer

YEARLING BOOKS are designed especially to entertain and enlighten young people. Patricia Reilly Giff, consultant to this series, received her bachelor's degree from Marymount College and a master's degree in history from St. John's University. She holds a Professional Diploma in Reading and a Doctorate of Humane Letters from Hofstra University. She was a teacher and reading consultant for many years, and is the author of numerous books for young readers.

Frozen Summer

Mary Jane Auch

A YEARLING BOOK

Published by
Dell Yearling
an imprint of
Random House Children's Books
a division of Random House, Inc.
1540 Broadway
New York, New York 10036

Visit us on the Web! www.randomhouse.com/kids

Educators and librarians, for a variety of teaching tools, visit us at www.randomhouse.com/teachers

ISBN: 0-440-41624-8

Reprinted by arrangement with Henry Holt and Company, Inc.

Printed in the United States of America

June 2000

10 9 8 7 6 5 4 3

OPM

Frozen Summer

# One

Mama left us for the first time on the sixth of June, 1816. It isn't hard to remember the date. Nobody in the Genesee Country of New York will ever forget the date, because it was different from every other June sixth that had ever been.

It all started with a scream that split the darkness and made me sit bolt upright in my bed. Had I been the one to cry out, or had it only been a dream? I held my breath, hearing nothing but the pounding of my own heart. If I had screamed, surely Mama or Papa would have heard me and climbed the ladder to see if I was all right. I envied my little brother, Joshua, sleeping downstairs between Papa and Mama's bed and the hearth instead of being alone in the cold cabin loft, shivering under two quilts like me.

The wind whispered through the cracks in the roof,

right over my head. I let out my breath and could see it
steaming—too cold for June. The murmuring of the wind
got louder, sounding almost like a person. Then I realized it wasn't the wind at all. It was Mama and Papa talking
in low voices. Suddenly Mama groaned, and Papa called,
"Mem! Wake up."

"I'm awake, Papa. What's wrong?"

"Just get dressed and come down here. Hurry, child."

The sound of alarm in my father's voice made my
fingers tremble and I could hardly tie the drawstring on
my dress. When I got downstairs, Papa was bundling a
still asleep Joshua into his heavy coat and woolen cap.
"Where are we going?" I asked.

Papa looked up. "You're not going anywhere. I need
you to stay with your mother while I go fetch Rebecca
Pierce. Your mother is . . . she's . . . unwell."

"What's wrong with her?" Mama was huddled under
the quilt, so I couldn't see her face. I hoped it wasn't the
ague. A number of settlers in the Genesee Country had
that disease, which gave them sudden fits of chills and
sweats, and for a few unlucky ones, a coffin.

"Jeremiah!" Mama cried out. "The baby will be here
before you leave the cabin!"

The baby! I had suspected Mama was going to have a
baby, but when I had asked her about it last month, she
just shushed me and said not to talk of such things. I had
no idea the baby would be coming this soon.

Papa fumbled with Joshua's mittens, then gave up and wrapped him in a quilt. "I'm starting out now, Aurelia. I'll leave Joshua at the Pierces'. Mem will stay with you."

"Papa, don't leave me alone with Mama. I don't know what to do."

"You'll be just fine, Mem. I'll be back directly with Rebecca Pierce. She's a midwife. She'll take care of everything."

Rebecca Pierce a midwife? Her daughter Hannah was my best friend, but she never had told me that. Worse yet, my own mother hadn't trusted me to know about the baby. And now here I was, only twelve years old and being left in charge of a birthing.

Joshua's head rolled against Papa's shoulder as Papa picked him up. I longed for Joshua's simple life. Nobody ever expected anything of him, and he could sleep through the most dire emergency.

Mama moaned in the bed and turned her face toward the wall. I didn't know if she cried out from pain or the thought of having to depend on only me while we waited.

I caught Papa's sleeve as he started out the door. "Papa, please!" I whispered. "Tell me what to do."

Papa stopped and looked over his shoulder. "Just talk to her, Mem."

"Talk? About what?"

"I don't know," Papa said, scowling. "Woman talk. The

women always gather around at birthings and talk. Just keep your mother calm."

Keeping Mama calm wasn't easy in the best of times. I knew I'd be hard pressed to soothe her now. As Papa went out the door, I could see why it had been so cold in the loft. Snow swirled around his ankles and into the room. What madness was this—a blizzard in June? I wished with all my heart we had never moved to the Genesee Country. We had been bound for disaster with our first steps. I shivered, but not from the cold.

As soon as the door slammed, Mama struggled out of bed.

"Mama, shouldn't you stay put until Mrs. Pierce gets here?"

She pulled a shawl around her shoulders. "We'll freeze if I don't get the fire burning. It's almost gone out."

The room was lit only by the flickering flame of one last log. Mama rolled it away from the embers that had been banked against the back wall of the hearth. The small pile of coals glowed red as she stirred them and pushed the log back in place with her shovel. Then she went to the woodbox. "There's no kindling. Did you forget to bring some in yesterday?"

"Yes, Mama. I'm sorry. I'll go gather some now." I'd been so busy helping Papa in the fields yesterday, I'd forgotten my housekeeping chores. Working out of doors made my heart sing, but I found no joy in housework. I pulled on my shoes and laced them up, then pushed the door open a crack. Snow rushed inside, swirling across the cabin floor. There were already several inches on the ground.

Mama looked over my shoulder. "You'll never find kindling in the dark under all that snow. I'll just put some small logs on the coals. If you fan them for me, they should catch." She gathered some logs from the woodbox, but just as she was about to put them on the coals, she gave out a cry and doubled over, letting the logs clatter across the hearth.

"Mama!" I ran to catch her, but I didn't see the water kettle and accidentally kicked it. I didn't have to look to know what I had done. I could hear the sharp hiss of water hitting hot coals as the room plunged into darkness.

"Mem!" Mama cried. "Quick! Save some of the coals."

"I will, Mama." I couldn't see anything in the darkness, so I knelt down on the hearth and felt through the wet coals until I found one that burned my finger. I pushed it to a dry spot and blew on it. Mama hovered over me with an unlit candle. "As soon as you get it going, light the candle with it. We'll use the flame to start the fire."

As I blew on the ember, it began to glow faintly. "It's coming, Mama. Don't worry. We'll have our fire." I blew again, and the coal shone bright for a second, then winked out like a distant star. No matter how hard I tried to help, I seemed to be making things worse.

"Oh, no!" Mama gasped. "Mem, how could you be so clumsy?" She bent over double again and started to cry in deep sobs that racked her whole body.

I took her arm and guided her to the bed. "I'll take care of you, Mama. Just lie down and rest."

She pulled away from me. "Rest! How can I rest? Even if Rebecca gets here in time, how will she see to deliver the babe?"

"Look, Mama, it's not so dark once your eyes get used to it." I wrapped the quilt around Mama's shoulders, then sat next to her, patting her back. "There must be a bright moon above the clouds. Look through the window. See how white the sky is?"

Mama buried her face in her hands. "I wish we were back in Connecticut. I need my mother and my sisters."

"I'm here, Mama. Just tell me what you need."

"I wish we'd never come here," Mama sobbed, ignoring my offer.

"I know," I whispered, but I knew she wasn't listening to me.

It had been all Papa's idea to leave our home and family to remove to the wilderness. He'd heard all the stories about the wonderful Genesee Country of New York, with land so fertile you could shove a broomstick in the ground and it would sprout leaves. But they turned out to be just that—stories. We had worked all summer and fall to get part of our land cleared and a cabin built. Then winter came, more bitter than any we'd ever seen in New England. Just when we thought it was over, we got more snow and hard frosts. Only two weeks ago, the sun finally shone high in the sky and warmed the earth. Papa and I had finished the plowing and planted the first of our corn. Yesterday those green sprouts were as tall as my thumb, but now they must be buried in snow.

Mama cried in pain and brought me out of my thoughts. "What can I do, Mama?"

"If you'd remembered the kindling," she snapped, "you could have built a fire."

"I'll try, Mama." The tinderbox was kept on the top shelf of the cupboard. As I ran my hands along the shelf, feeling for it, I tipped over the crock that held the last of our dried peas. I could hear them skittering across the floor in all directions.

"Oh, Mem," Mama moaned. "Just sit down and try to stay out of trouble."

"I'll pick up the peas as soon as I have the fire lit, Mama. I've found the tinderbox."

My hands were trembling from the cold as I tried to open the tin box. I pulled hard on the lid and the contents started to spill out, but I wasn't about to drop anything else. I made a grab and felt the fragile char cloth turn to a handful of flakes in my hand. I could still have used the crumbled flakes to start the fire, but I knew I'd never find them in the darkness. I struck the flint with the steel and showered sparks down on the logs, but I knew it wasn't going to work. I needed something that would take the spark and burst into flames. I needed tinder, and it was my own fault that I had none.

Then I remembered. "We'll have light when Papa comes back, Mama. He'll have the lantern on the sleigh."

Mama sighed. "Look out the door and see if your father is in sight yet."

I knew there hadn't been time for Papa to go all the way to the Pierces' and back. It took me the better part of an hour to walk to Hannah's in good weather. Since we didn't have a horse, Papa had to hitch the oxen to the wagon to fetch Mrs. Pierce, and they didn't walk much faster than I did. "It's too soon, Mama."

"It's going to be too late!" Mama cried. "The baby is coming shortly. Go outside and watch for them."

I wrapped a shawl around my shoulders and pushed open the door. The wind threw stinging ice crystals into my face, almost snatching my breath away. I cupped my hands around my eyes, searching for the glow of Papa's lantern, but all around me there was nothing but a swirling blanket of white. "Papa!" I screamed. "Papa!" The only answer was the howling of the wind.

I tried to remember what I knew of birthings. Five years ago, when Joshua was born, I was only seven years old. During all the excitement, one of our neighbors took me up to my room and told me stories, so I knew nothing of what was going on downstairs. Later, when we had come downstairs, Mama had a little wiggly crea-

ture wrapped in a blanket. Papa had laughed when I
blurted, "Mama, did we get a puppy?" I had been more
than a little disappointed to find out it was only a baby
brother.

Now I stood shivering in the cold, not wanting to go
into the cabin. Why did Mama treat me as if I were a stupid clumsy fool? That wasn't fair. On the journey from
Connecticut to the Genesee Country I'd been separated
from the family for three days and managed just fine,
even when I met up with a mountain lion. And after we
settled here, I'd been the one to save our cow, Chloe,
from a bear. Papa had even confided in me that I seemed
better suited to pioneer life than Mama. And now she
acted as if I were useless.

Even though I was afraid, I knew I could help with the
birthing. After all, I'd seen Papa help Chloe give birth to
her calf and I'd seen a cat give birth to kittens. The wind
slipped icy fingers of snow down my neck and my teeth
clattered together, finally forcing me to go inside.

Mama appeared to be sleeping. At first I sat next to
her, but I was so cold my shivering shook the whole bed,
and I thought I might wake her. I went around to the
other side and slipped under the quilt, moving slowly so
as not to make the rope bed frame creak. Every now and
then, Mama would moan and shift position, but then her
breathing would get slow and even again. I tried not to
move, praying that she would stay asleep until Papa got
back with Mrs. Pierce.

I must have fallen asleep myself because Mama's cry awoke me. "Mem, where are you? I need you."

I jumped out of bed and ran to the other side. Mama was struggling to sit up. "Take my hand and help me, please."

It was so dark, I could barely see anything, but I knelt on the bed in front of her and pulled her up. "Just tell me what you need, Mama," I said. "I'll do everything you say."

She gripped my hand. "Push against my knee, Mem." I didn't know what she meant. "No!" she cried. "This isn't working. We need more people."

"Papa will be back with Mrs. Pierce, Mama. Just try to wait until she gets here."

"Wait!" Mama shrieked. "I can't wait. This baby wants to come now. Help pull me up in the bed so I can lean against the wall."

I scrambled around behind her and managed to help her into position.

"That's better," she said. "Now I should have one person on each side of me, but we'll have to do our best."

"I don't understand what you need, Mama."

"When the next pains come, push hard against my knee, and give me your other hand to pull on."

"But I don't see what you . . ."

"Now!" Mama cried. She gripped my hand and pulled, but that made her start sliding down in the bed again. Now I understood what she needed. By pushing against her knee, I could keep her braced so her back stayed against the wall. She pulled so hard this time, I felt like a bow being drawn by an archer. Then she relaxed, breathing hard. "That's good, Mem. Do it just like that, each time."

"Each time?" I wondered how many times there would be.

"Yes. Now!"

She struggled again and again with a shorter time in between each push. Although I couldn't make out her face in the darkness, I could tell she was getting tired and weaker. Babies were much harder to get born than kittens. I only hoped they came easier than a calf.

"Just a few more pushes," Mama gasped.

I was still frightened, but I was proud that I could help Mama. After all, up until tonight, Mama had thought me too young to even know about the baby. Now I was becoming a midwife. Mama had just started to push again when the door flew open and we were blinded by the light of a lantern.

"Oh, Rebecca, thank heaven you're here!" Mama cried.

Rebecca Pierce rushed into the room with Hannah and her older sister, Mercy. They shook the snow from their coats and bonnets. "All right," Mrs. Pierce said, fastening her wet hair back with a comb, "Jeremiah, bring the light over here, then fetch those coals from the foot warmers in the sleigh and get us a fire going." She looked at me. "Get out of the way now, Mem."

"Come on, Hannah," I said, pulling on my best friend's arm. I couldn't wait to tell her about what had happened. Since she was the youngest in her family, I was sure she knew less about birthings than I did.

"I can't," Hannah said.

"Why not?" I whispered. "I have so much to tell you."

"I'm sorry, Mem. My mother needs me to help."

Mama cried out again. Mrs. Pierce looked over her shoulder. "Hannah, get over here. Mem, you'd best get up in the loft. We have work to do."

I looked to Papa for support. He thought of me as a helper, not a child who gets in the way. But Papa was in the far corner of the room, trying to stay out of the way himself.

Tears stung my eyes as I climbed the ladder. I crouched by the opening in the floor and looked down to the scene below. As Papa got the fire going, the room glowed with an orange light. Mrs. Pierce and her daughters crowded around Mama so I couldn't see her. Hannah had climbed onto the bed behind Mama and was holding her up in a sitting position. Mercy and Mrs. Pierce each took one of her hands and pushed against her knees, as I had been doing. I heard the murmur of their voices, but not their words.

Mama's cries grew louder. Then suddenly there was a new voice in the room—the lusty howl of a new babe. Mrs. Pierce lifted the baby, all shiny and steaming in the cold cabin. There was some sort of cord attached to him.

Mrs. Pierce tied a string around it, then cut it. I had seen a cord like that before with the birthing of kittens.

Mrs. Pierce handed the baby to Hannah, who deftly cleaned him and swaddled him in a cloth. Hannah was three months younger than me, but it seemed she knew exactly how to help at a birthing. I was being banished to the upstairs again, just like when Joshua was born. Only this time, there was nobody to tell me stories.

"Let me see him," Mama said. "Is he healthy?"

I watched as Hannah took the babe over to Mama. Mama kissed the top of his head, then undid the wrappings. She moaned softly, letting her head drop back on the pillow, then looked over at Papa. "I'm sorry, Jeremiah."

Papa rushed to her side, looked at the baby, then shook his head. "It's not your fault, Aurelia. It can't be helped."

"What's wrong?" I called. "May I come down now?"

Mama mumbled something I couldn't hear.

"Please?" I cried. "May I come see the baby?"

Nobody answered, but I didn't care. I scrambled down the ladder and ran over to the bed, my feet almost sliding out from under me on some of the peas I had spilled.

"Remembrance," Mama said, "slow down before you cause any more damage." Mama always called me by my full name when she was annoyed with me.

"I just want to see the baby." Mama made no move to show him to me, so I leaned over and lifted the flap of the blanket. There, looking up at me, was the sweetest little face I had ever seen.

"He looks perfect," I whispered.

"There's only one thing wrong with him," Mama said, speaking so softly I could barely hear her. "He's a girl."

"A girl? May I hold her?" Mama didn't answer. She stared straight ahead—not looking at me or the baby. There was an expression on her face that I'd never seen before. When Joshua was born, Mama had been so happy, she cried. And she couldn't get enough of looking at his face and kissing his tiny fingers. "Look, Mem," she had said. "Look at your little brother. Isn't he beautiful?"

But now, Mama might as well have been holding a sack of cornmeal for all the attention she gave the baby, which squirmed, getting one of her hands loose from the blanket. I touched the hand, marveling at the tiny perfect fingernails. "Mama, see how lovely she is."

Mama didn't even look at the baby. She just stared straight up at the ceiling, as if she were alone in the room.

Mrs. Pierce put her arm around me. "Leave your mama be for a while, Mem. She needs to rest."

I had a feeling that something was terribly wrong with Mama and rest wasn't going to help.

Two

The Pierces stayed the better part of the day, tending to Mama and the baby. Hannah's responsibilities were over, so she and I had time to talk up in the loft. It felt so good to see Hannah again. A new teacher had opened the summer session of school in the beginning of April, but in a few weeks, she became so homesick for her family, she moved back home to Canandaigua and school was closed. Between Mama keeping me busy with chores and the nasty weather, Hannah and I had hardly seen each other since then.

"There's a new teacher coming next week," Hannah said. "Did you hear about that? The school board decided to keep school open, even though many of the students will still be helping with the late planting."

"How would I hear about a new teacher?" I said.

"Nobody ever tells me anything. My best friend doesn't even tell me her mother is a midwife."

Hannah shrugged. "It just never came up, Mem. We always had other things to talk about. Besides, this is the first birth we've attended since you came here, and I've only been to three before today."

"You've helped deliver three other babies? Who?"

Hannah thought for a minute. "Emmeline Porter's baby is the only one you know."

I remembered the infant Mrs. Porter had brought to our cabin raising. The Porters had come to help us on the day after their own cabin had burned to the ground. Then, a few weeks later, we'd helped at their cabin raising. That's the way things worked in the wilderness. Neighbors depended on each other for help.

"You have no call to be vexed at me for keeping secrets," Hannah said. "You never told me your mother was expecting a baby."

"That's because I didn't know." The words had tumbled out of my mouth before I realized how ridiculous they would sound. "I mean, I suspected, but when I asked Mama, she said I shouldn't talk about such things."

Hannah laughed. "Oh, Mem, even if your mama didn't tell you, you'd have to know. I suspected your mama was going to have a baby when we came to visit last month. She was wearing her apron high. Didn't you notice?"

I ignored her question. There was no need to make myself look even more stupid than I already had. "Why didn't you say something if you knew your mother would be the midwife?"

"I didn't know until your papa came to fetch us. There's another midwife in Pultneyville. She could have been using her. I'm sure Mama knew ahead of time, but she never tells me anything, either."

That made me feel a little better. Mama wasn't the only mother who didn't share her thoughts with her daughter.

"One thing makes me really angry," I said. "Why should Mama and Papa be upset about the baby being a girl? I'd rather have a girl baby than a boy baby any day."

"You know why, Mem. The boys can help with the heavy work."

"So can girls. I can handle our team of oxen as well as any man. I even heard Papa brag about it to your pa once. Besides, I'm glad I have a little sister."

Hannah smiled. "I hope she's more fun than a big sister. I wonder if Mercy was glad when I was born."

"Mercy was certainly on her good behavior today. She didn't say one nasty thing to us." That was worthy of comment because Mercy Pierce was one of the nastiest girls I had ever met.

"Of course not. She's always Miss Perfect when adults are around."

"Are you talking about anyone I know?" Mercy had climbed the ladder to the loft and was glaring at us, only her head and shoulders visible above the floor.

"Not unless you know somebody perfect," Hannah said.

"Mama wants you children to come downstairs. We're having a hot meal before we go home."

Mercy spat out the word *children* just to annoy us, but Hannah and I were hungry, so we held our tongues and followed her back downstairs. Mrs. Pierce had made a stew of carrots, potatoes, and a rabbit that they must have brought with them. We had been out of meat for more than two months, except for a tiny bit of salt pork that Mama saved for special occasions. Papa wasn't a hunter, and a bear had killed the pregnant sow that would have given us feeder pigs by now.

Papa came in just in time for the meal, stamping the snow from his boots at the door. "How has your crop fared in the weather, Jeremiah?" Mrs. Pierce asked.

"The corn is still under the cover of the snow," Papa said. "I'll know when it melts if the snow kept it from being killed by the frost."

"Wouldn't the snow be cold enough to kill the corn, Papa?" I asked.

"Not necessarily," Papa said through a mouthful of stew. "If the snow fell fast enough, it could have acted like a blanket, protecting the plants from the cold air. We'll just have to wait and see."

While we ate at the table, Mrs. Pierce stayed at Mama's bedside, trying to coax her into taking a few sips of the broth from the stew. When they were ready to leave, Mrs. Pierce took me aside. "Try to get your mama to eat, Mem. She needs plenty of sleep, too, to get her strength back. And when the babe cries, take her to your mama to be nursed. Mind you keep the fire going when it's cold like this. I declare I've never seen a stranger spring."

Hannah put on her cloak and bonnet and gave me a hug. "I'm so glad school is starting again, Mem. You'll be coming, won't you? I mean after the snow stops."

"I'll be there," I said. I might have to work extra hard on chores at night, but surely Mama wouldn't want me to miss out on my schooling. Many girls my age stopped going to school, but I was going to be a teacher and needed all the learning I could get.

Both Mama and the baby were sleeping by the time Papa left with the Pierces. I fussed around the cabin, sweeping up the last of the dried peas I'd spilled and washing the dishes from our meal. I kept tiptoeing over to the cradle to peek at my sister. She looked like an angel, with a fringe of dark eyelashes resting on her rosy cheeks.

Finally I couldn't resist picking up the baby. I was careful to hold her head the way Mama had shown me with Joshua. I rested her against my shoulder and could feel her stirring, snuggling in against my neck. "I think it's just fine that you're a girl," I whispered. "As soon as you're old enough to walk, you can help me drive the team.

I'm afraid Mama will still make you learn all those boring sewing skills—especially embroidery. What a foolish waste of time."

I kissed the baby on the top of her fuzzy head and laid her gently in the cradle. Suddenly her eyes opened and she began to cry. I tried rocking her, but that only made her cry louder. Mama turned over in the bed. "What's wrong with it?"

It? She called the baby "it"? We'd have to name this baby soon. I'd bring that up when Mama was in good spirits again.

"I think the baby is hungry, Mama. Mrs. Pierce said I should bring her to you to be nursed when she cried."

I lifted the baby from her crib and took her to Mama. Mama turned away.

"Just walk around with the baby, Mem. It'll go back to sleep."

I paced back and forth across the cabin until my feet had worn a path in the dirt floor. I tried humming softly, but the baby couldn't hear me over her screams. I tried bouncing her up and down a little. Mama used to do that with Joshua, and it made him giggle. This baby wasn't giggling. I tried swinging her in my arms like a cradle, but the crying continued.

"Oh, for heaven's sake," Mama said finally. "Bring it here."

She took the baby in her arms and nursed her, but

there was no look of tenderness on her face the way there had been with Joshua.

I decided something had to be done, and I wasn't going to wait until Mama was in a good mood. That could take forever. "Mama, what are we going to name the baby?"

"It's too soon for a name," Mama said.

"Too soon? Why?"

"Not many babies survive in the wilderness. We'll name it when we know if it's going to live. Probably be a blessing if it doesn't." She stared off into space, never even glancing at the child she was nursing.

"Mama, are you angry because the baby isn't a boy? Because if you are, that's not fair. Girls can be just as much help as boys."

Mama turned to me, her eyes flashing. For the first time today, she looked like herself again, but it wasn't the self I was hoping to see. "You think I'm upset not to have a boy to work in the fields? I'd be glad to have a girl to help me with household chores, since the daughter I have would rather be running around with a team of oxen. Heaven knows, I could use the help."

"Then what is it, Mama?"

"What do you think this child's future will be, Mem? She'll grow up and get married. Then her husband will take some foolish notion to move to some godforsaken spot where there's nothing but trees, and neighbors are

more than an hour's walk away. You'll do the same thing,
Mem—follow some lunking farmer to the wilds of Ohio
or even beyond."

"I won't marry and go off, Mama. I'll always be here
with you and Papa. I'm going to be a teacher, remember?"

Mama was clutching the baby so tight in her arms that
the poor thing stopped nursing and started to cry again.
Mama stared past me. "Oh, you'll marry, all right. And
you'll leave just as sure as you're standing here now.
You'll desert me the way I left my mama and my sisters."
She pushed her head back on the pillow and sobbed
along with the baby.

I stood watching her for a minute, not knowing what
to do. I reached to touch Mama's shoulder, but she
turned away, half rolling on the baby. I backed away and
sat on the stool by the fire, ready to rescue the baby if
Mama accidentally hurt her.

How I wished we'd never left Connecticut. My
grandma would know what to do. She'd love the baby
even if Mama didn't. I reached for the chain of the locket
that I always wore hidden under my dress. Grandma had
given it to me just before we started off from home. The
locket was a secret between Grandma and me. It had
been given to her by her grandma, and we were all three
named Remembrance. I held the locket in my palm, tilt-
ing it so the reflection of the fireplace flames made the
gold gleam in the darkness of the cabin. I ran my finger

over the curved lines of the lily design on its surface. That's when I decided what to name the baby.

Just then there was a sharp cry and I could see the baby's little fists flailing above the blanket. I rushed over and Mama thrust the bundle toward me. "Here, take the baby. It's had enough." I didn't even have time to cradle the baby's head before Mama let go and burrowed back under the covers. I clutched at the baby, and her fists flew up again, startled.

"There, there," I whispered, hugging her. "It's all right." I went back to the stool by the fire and rocked forward and back, the baby snuggled into my shoulder. We'd had to leave behind our old rocking chair because it didn't fit into the wagon. I could rock the baby without it, but I missed the rhythmic squeak that used to put me to sleep when Mama had nursed Joshua in the room we had shared.

"You need a name," I whispered into the tiny ear. "And even if Mama doesn't want to give you one yet, I'm going to have my own name for you. From now on, you're Lily—Lily Nye. It's perfect, because lilies are soft and beautiful."

Gradually, I could feel Lily relax. "Don't worry, Lily," I whispered. "Mem will take care of you."

It surprised me to hear how much "Mem" sounded like "Mama."

Three

Mama perked up some when Papa brought Joshua back from the Pierces' farm.

"Can I see him, Mama?" Joshua shouted as he came through the door. "Can I see the baby?"

"Bring the babe over to me, Mem," Mama said. She reached out and smiled when I handed Lily to her, then pulled back the edge of the blanket so Joshua could see the baby's face. "This is your new sister, Joshua."

Joshua stretched his upper body across the bed and shoved his nose into Lily's waving fist. "Look, she caught my nose. Let go my nose, baby." He looked at Mama. "What's her name?"

"You can call her 'baby' for now."

"Hello, baby," he said, grinning at Lily. I was glad to see that somebody in the family besides me was happy to have Lily join us.

❧

"The snow has melted off some," Papa said after breakfast the next morning. "We should be able to tell if our crop survived."

"May I go, too, Papa?" I asked.

"If your mama doesn't need you. Will you be all right, Aurelia?"

Mama nodded. "Just don't go running off, Mem. I'm still feeling poorly. I'll need you to clean up the breakfast dishes and put some dinner on before long."

"I will, Mama. I'll fix us a good meal."

I wrapped myself in Mama's shawl. It had warmed enough for the snow to have melted in the open spaces, but the sky hung low over us like a wet wool blanket on a clothesline. Papa and I walked the long path to the cornfield. It didn't seem like much of a field by New England standards, with all the stumps of trees still standing. Everything had to be done fast in the wilderness. Chop down trees and plow around their stumps instead of taking the time to pull them out. Then gather everyone to put up a cabin in a day or two. Since we arrived, it had been a race against time—a race against the winds and snows of winter. And now winter wouldn't let go of us.

When the cornfield came into view, I could see that only a few patches of snow remained, but I couldn't see the corn. It wasn't until we got close that I saw the plants, blackened and limp, curled into the thawing ground.

Papa squatted in the field and pulled up one of the seedlings. "Look at the roots on this plant. This would have been a vigorous crop." He tossed it aside and stood. "I'll have to see if I can buy some seed corn from one of our neighbors. George Pierce told me he had a good crop last year. He should be able to spare me some. I need seed potatoes, too."

"Do you want me to help you, Papa? School is starting again on Monday, but I'll stay home if you need me."

"You helped with the plowing, Mem. I can get the seed in by myself. Your mama is going to need you now."

"Yes, Papa," I said, but I knew I couldn't bear the thought of being cooped up in the cabin. I hoped that Mama would be doing well enough by Monday to release me. I had three days to get her up and going again, or at least well enough to be left alone.

I searched along the edge of the field for the fiddle-heads and leeks that had started sprouting in the past few weeks, but the cold must have killed them off. Mama had been looking forward to a good meal of spring greens. Now we were back to cornmeal mush, and not a lot of that left, either.

When we returned to the house, Papa walked on to the Pierces' to inquire about seed corn while I went inside. Mama seemed more her old self again, counting Lily's fingers and toes with Joshua.

"You're feeling better, Mama?" I asked.

She smiled—a most welcome sight. "Yes, Mem. Much better. I'm hungry, though. I'd like some more of that stew, if there is any."

"There's enough for one serving, Mama. I'll fix it for you."

"No, never mind. Save it for your father. He'll need strength for the hard work he's doing."

"Birthing a baby is hard work, Mama. You need the food now more than Papa does."

Mama nodded and looked pleased at my remark.

I spent the rest of that day and the next fussing over Mama, plumping her pillows and fluffing out her quilts. I cleaned every inch of the cabin, even sweeping the dirt floor in a design of wavy lines, though Joshua quickly made a mess of that. "It pleases me to see you taking an interest in women's work, Mem," Mama said, more than once. If she only knew I was just doing it to get her into good spirits so I could escape to school in the morning, she wouldn't be so pleased. I felt a small pang of guilt for my deception.

When the sun warmed the air on Sunday, I wrapped Mama in her shawl and helped her walk outside for a bit. We went slowly around the cabin, then out toward the field. I was chattering on about nothing just to be cheerful, when Mama stopped and put her hand on my arm. "Listen."

We stayed quiet for a minute and heard nothing.

"What was it, Mama?"

Mama sighed. "For a moment I thought I heard church bells."

"It couldn't have been, Mama. There are no churches around here. When the circuit rider comes through to preach, he just holds meetings in people's houses."

"I know," Mama said. "It's just that I miss the sound of church bells. Doesn't seem like Sunday, not going to church. I'm getting tired now. You'd best help me back to the cabin."

On the way back, Mama looked at the small garden patch along the fence where she had planted sweet peas the month before. I tried to steer her away, sure that they had been killed by the snow, but Mama insisted on going there. A small patch of snow still clung to the spot that was shaded by the cabin.

"Push aside the snow, Mem."

"But Mama . . ." I couldn't stand to see her get all melancholy again. Those seeds were the ones Grandma had given her to plant in the new land. I knew Mama looked on them as a sign of good luck, and now she'd find them limp, like the corn.

"Don't make me get down there and clear it away myself, Mem."

"Yes, Mama." I crouched and pushed the wet snow from the patch. There under their icy cover were bright yellow-green leaves just breaking through the ground.

Mama beamed. "I knew they'd make it. That's why

sweet peas are your grandmother's favorite flower. They wait patiently under the snow and break forth with the first warm day."

The sweet peas must have cast a good luck charm on me because that night Mama decided I should go to school the next morning. "It's important, Jeremiah," she told Papa. "If she's to be a teacher, Mem needs all the schooling she can get. Besides, who knows how long this teacher will last? If she leaves like the last one, there might be no schooling till the winter session."

Papa finally agreed, and I took my freshly washed dress from the rack in front of the fire and ironed it. I had to reheat the iron many times by the fire to finish the task, but my dress looked almost as crisp as new when I was done with it. Then I brushed my hair a hundred strokes, the way Mama had taught me. I wanted to make a good impression on my first day with our new teacher.

Monday morning at dawn, I started on the long walk to school. Much of the snow had melted off, making the road rutted and muddy. Another frost during the night had made a coating of ice, which crunched when I stepped on it. I had to keep hopping from one dry spot to another to keep from soaking my shoes. Before long, I could feel the big toes on each foot rubbing against the leather. Mama was right about me growing fast this winter—right at least about my feet. The rubbing finally got so painful, I stopped and took off my stockings and shoes. I tied the laces together and slung the shoes over my shoulder. The frosting of ice on the mud felt sharp on my feet, but it was better than blisters. The pail of corn cakes I carried for lunch was still warm. I thought for a moment about warming my feet on the outside of the pail, but decided that muddy footprints wouldn't make my lunch seem very appetizing.

My feet were altogether numb by the time I came to the crossroads in Williamson. I looked down the road to see if Hannah and her brothers and sisters were coming, but they were nowhere in sight. I ran the last few feet to the schoolhouse and headed right for the fireplace. I tucked my lunch tin into a pile of warm ashes and stayed there, toasting my feet on the hearth stones.

From the corner of my eye, I spied the teacher at her desk, surrounded by a group of students. She had maple syrup–colored hair just like mine. I wondered how long it would take this teacher to get homesick for her family and abandon us. I couldn't blame anyone for wanting to leave, especially a summer session teacher. There were too many farm chores that kept students from attending school this time of year, especially when most would be doing their planting all over again because of the frost.

"Mem! I didn't see you come in." Hannah broke away from the group at the teacher's desk and joined me by the fireplace. "What happened to your shoes?"

"My feet decided to grow this morning."

Hannah lined her foot up against mine. Her feet were

at least a big toenail longer than mine. "I have a pair of shoes at home you can have. I just outgrew them and got Mercy's pair. My feet are sliding around inside hers, but it's better than being pinched. My old ones should fit you just fine. But we shouldn't have to wear shoes much longer anyway."

"If spring ever comes," I said.

Hannah glanced back over to the new teacher. "Will you look at Royal talking to Miss Becher? He's only known her since yesterday afternoon, and he's acting like a lovesick calf."

Royal, the youngest of Hannah's brothers, was beet red with pleasure. "How did he meet her yesterday?"

"She's boarding with us all month. Mama says she'll feed this one so well and keep her so busy, she won't have time to get homesick."

"Why is the teacher boarding with your family?"

"It was our turn. We hadn't had a teacher since last year. You'll probably get her next, since you haven't done it yet."

I tried to picture where a teacher would sleep in our house. Up in the loft with me?

"What are you frowning about?" Hannah asked.

"I just never heard of that—a teacher living with her students. Our teacher in Connecticut lived with her family."

"Well, our teachers come from outside the town, and the school doesn't pay them enough to get a house, especially the women. Besides, there aren't any extra houses. A teacher would have to be rich enough to have one built for her."

We didn't have time to discuss the matter, because Miss Becher made us take our seats. Hannah could have had a choice spot near the fireplace in the front with her sister, Mercy, because their father donated more firewood to the school than any of the other fathers, but she chose to sit near the back with me. With all the building and such, Papa hadn't had time to cut extra firewood. The only ones behind us were Leonard and Henry Crowell, whose father said any firewood he cut would go to warm his family, not some thin-blooded city schoolmarm.

I didn't pay much attention to what we were supposed to be learning that morning, because I was making a study of Miss Becher. She didn't look much older than Mercy—eighteen at the most—with a sweet face and pale gray eyes. When I became a teacher in six more years, would I have to board out with the families of my pupils? What if I had to live with people I didn't like? Would I have no choice in the matter? Would I get homesick and run away like the last teacher?

Hannah's elbow in my ribs made me aware that Miss Becher was calling my name. "Would you read the next passage for us, Remembrance Nye?" Hannah handed the book to me, pointing to the place where I was supposed to be reading.

I stammered and struggled over words that I knew as well as my own name. When I became a teacher, I'd never make my pupils read aloud. Leonard Crowell snorted behind me. I took a deep breath and started again. I could feel Leonard's foot on the leg of our bench and his laughter made it shake, so the words on the page got even more jumbled.

"That will be quite enough, Leonard," Miss Becher said. "I'll not have you laughing at Remembrance because she has difficulty with her reading."

"But I read very well," I said. "I plan to be a teacher someday."

The minute the words were out of my mouth, I regretted them. Leonard's older brother, Henry, jumped up and bowed to me. "Good morning, Miz Teacher. How come you cain't read, Miz Teacher?"

Miss Becher slapped her ruler down on our bench right in front of him, but it scared Hannah and me far more than it did Henry. Then Leonard chimed in. "How come you ain't got no shoes on, Miz Teacher? I ain't never heard of a barefoot teacher."

Both Henry and Leonard towered over Miss Becher. She looked frightened for just a second. Then she swatted both of them right on the head with her ruler. They yelped and scrambled back into their seats. "I'll not have any of you making fun of another pupil who is less fortunate. If I ever see that behavior from either one of you again, I'll . . ." Her voice trailed off, as if she wasn't used to thinking up punishments and probably not very good at delivering them.

I felt my face burn. "I'm not less fortunate," I said. "My feet just grew is all."

At that, Henry couldn't hold back his laughter. He exploded and sprayed spit all over the back of my neck.

The rest of the school day was just as bad as the beginning. I had put my lunch tin into coals that were too hot, so when I opened it, the cornmeal mush was charred and stuck to the bottom. When Miss Becher asked me to recite my sums that afternoon, I couldn't remember a single one. By the end of the day, she was looking at me with sympathy, as if she thought me dull witted and beyond help. Then the Crowell brothers walked two miles out of their way to taunt me as I walked home.

But that wasn't the worst of it. When I got back home and opened our cabin door, Lily was crying and Joshua was rocking her cradle, trying to comfort her. Tearstains streaked his dirty cheeks. "Mem!" he cried, running to me. He grabbed me around the legs, burying his face in my skirts. "The baby . . . is sad," he cried, his words coming out in little hiccups. "I can't . . . make her . . . happy."

"But where's Mama, Joshua? Did she leave you alone?"

I followed his trembling finger and saw her. She sat in the shadows, staring, unhearing.

When I looked into her eyes, I could tell that Mama had left us again.

Four

I dropped my lunch pail and went to Mama, putting one hand on her shoulder. She didn't seem to notice my touch. "Mama, are you all right?"

She started rocking forward and back on the stool, her hands clenched in her lap.

Joshua pulled at my sleeve. "Mem, fix the baby. Please! Make the baby happy." Lily's screams filled the cabin, and I suddenly had the horrible thought that Mama might have hurt her. I ran over and knelt by Lily's cradle. Her face was dark red from the crying. I unwrapped her from the swaddling cloth and gently moved her arms and legs, but the crying got neither better nor worse, so I couldn't tell if she'd been hurt or was only frightened. I knew Mama would never hurt her on purpose, but I also knew Mama wasn't right in her mind.

I picked Lily up, but instead of nestling against my

shoulder, she stiffened, screaming even harder. "It's all right, Lily. Shhh. Everything's all right." I stroked her back, because I knew she couldn't hear me over her wailing. Joshua was crying now, too, needing comforting as much as Lily. I sat on the stool by the hearth and held out my free arm. He rushed over and clung to me, sobbing into my coat. I rocked in the chair, keeping my eye on Mama, following her rhythm. Still she only stared, not seeing any of us.

I nuzzled Joshua's hair with my cheek and pulled him closer to me. "Joshua, calm yourself. I need to know what happened. What started Lily crying?"

"Because of Mama," he said, his words muffled by my coat.

"Did Mama hurt the baby?" I whispered.

"No . . . she just . . ." He turned and waved his pudgy fingers toward Mama, having no words to explain.

I felt strange, talking to Joshua like this in front of Mama, but I had to find out what had happened. "Can you remember how long Mama's been sitting there, Joshua?"

He took in a big gasp of air and shuddered. "Papa came in for dinner and then went back to the field."

"And Mama has been like that ever since?" For the first time I noticed the table covered with dirty dishes.

Joshua nodded, his chin quivered, and his eyes filled with new tears. I looked at the hearth. The fire had almost gone out. Lily's blanket was soaked near through, and she still screamed. I couldn't handle this alone. "Do you think you could go to the field and get Papa for me by yourself, Joshua?"

"I think so."

"All right. Tell him Mama is sick and we need him to come right away."

I laid Lily down in her cradle and bundled Joshua into his warm jacket and wool cap. "Now mind you don't dawdle. Just follow the path straight out to the field." I went outside with him. We could see Papa in the distance, tossing rocks onto the wooden sled. "There he is, Joshua."

I watched Joshua run down the path. He stopped and turned three times to wave to me. When I was sure he was really heading for Papa, I went back into the cabin and found a clean blanket and clouts for Lily. I was afraid I'd pierce her with the straight pin when I fastened them. Somehow I managed to weave the pin in and out of the cloth without taking any skin, in spite of my trembling fingers and her thrashing legs. I wrapped her tight into the blanket after I changed her, and she seemed to calm some.

I took Lily over to Mama. "The baby needs feeding, Mama." I tried to put Lily in her arms, but she wouldn't unclench her hands. "Mama!" I said, shaking her shoulder. "The baby is hungry. You must feed her. Come back to the bed. You'll be more comfortable there." Lily's cries started up again.

I pulled at Mama's hands until they came unclasped, then grabbed her by the wrist and tugged at her until she stood. Once she was on her feet, Mama followed me meekly over to the bed and climbed in. "Here," I said, placing Lily in her arms. "Please feed her, Mama. She needs you." I tried to force a gentleness into my voice that I didn't feel. How could Mama let her frightened children cry all afternoon?

Mama looked at Lily, and her face softened. "Feed her, Mama," I said again, quietly this time.

Mama's eyes met mine. She nodded, then arranged her clothes and began nursing Lily.

As soon as I was sure everything was all right, I went over to the hearth, stirred up the coals, and put on another log, fanning it with a turkey wing to get it to flame up. Smoke swirled around the room, stinging my eyes. That was one of the things I hated most about an open hearth. The smoke didn't rise up the chimney until the fire got going hard. I moved the water kettle closer to the fire, then went back to Mama. Lily was still nursing peacefully.

"Should I wash the wet clouts, Mama? I can't remember what we used to do with Joshua's when he was a baby."

"Only wash them if they're soiled," Mama said. "The wet ones can just be dried and used again."

I put the clouts on the rack next to the fire. The smell soon reminded me of when Joshua had been a baby. I decided from now on, I'd rinse them out before drying, even if they were only wet. It was bad enough that we lived in a house with manure in the chinking of the walls that reeked during a long wet spell. We needn't add baby smells to it.

After I swept the floor, I went over to check on Mama and Lily. "Are you better now, Mama?"

"Some better," she said. "I was feeling poorly today." A tear ran down her cheek. "At home, this would be my sitting-up week."

I sat on the edge of the bed. "I don't know what you mean, Mama."

Mama's face had a wistful expression. "Don't you remember? The first week after a baby was born, the neighbor women all came to call. They brought cakes and even dishes to serve at dinner. I'd have my good china out for tea."

I suddenly had a vision of Mama receiving guests in the sitting room at home. Papa and my uncles had moved the big bed downstairs for her. She had looked like a queen with a special bed jacket Grandma had fashioned for her with lavender ribbons all down the front. The bed was made up with her wedding quilt and pillows with crocheted lace. She had Joshua in a cradle by her bed and her good tea set on a table on the other side. The house filled every afternoon with friends who had come to admire Joshua, and they all brought wonderful confections for tea. I remembered a cake with strawberries and whipped cream so well, I could almost taste its sweetness on my tongue. It was no wonder that Mama longed to be back in Connecticut.

I came out of my daydream and looked around the dark, smoky cabin. A small barrel in the corner held Mama's precious tea set still packed in sawdust. There had been no reason to take it out since we'd come here. Mama looked small and helpless in the rough-hewn bed with everyday quilts and plain cases. The fancy linens had been left in Connecticut to be sent for when they were needed, but the need never arose. They would seem out of place in this simple cabin.

I moved to the head of the bed and leaned down to kiss Mama's forehead. "It will be all right, Mama. It's just different here."

"I need my sisters and my mother," Mama said, her voice breaking.

"Then we'll write and tell them about the baby, Mama. Maybe Grandma could even come for a visit. She could be here in less than a week if she came by stagecoach."

Mama smiled through her tears. "That would be wonderful. I've missed her so much."

"I'll find some paper and we can write to her now, Mama. That will make you feel better. Maybe she can bring some real tea from home." The settlers around us used something called "Oswego tea," but it didn't taste anything like what we had at home. Mama loved tea, but even when some came into the general store in

Williamson, which wasn't very often, it cost too dear for her to buy it. We could get coffee or sugar for three shillings a pound, but a pound of tea was twelve shillings. There were many things we needed far worse than tea.

I heard Papa's voice outside and suddenly felt guilty for calling him in from the field. After all, I had been able to make Mama feel better by myself. Papa burst into the room with Joshua at his heels. "What's all this? Are you ill, Aurelia? Do you need me to fetch the doctor?"

"No, Jeremiah. I just had a spell is all. I'm much better now." Her eyes were bright with tears, but she smiled. "I'm going to write a letter to my mother and see if she'll come for a visit. Don't you think that's a fine idea?"

Papa took off his hat and wiped his forehead with the sleeve of his jacket. "We've no place to put her, Aurelia, and barely enough food to get us through to the first harvest. I can't see how we'd put up a guest."

"But family doesn't count as guests, Jeremiah, and my mother doesn't eat very much. I really need her to come."

Papa frowned. "By the time your mother could get here, you'd be back on your feet again. Mem can help you for the next few days. It won't hurt her to miss a bit of school."

Papa cut himself a slice of bread from the table and frowned again, this time at the dirty dishes. He didn't see the smile fade from Mama's face. "You're all right now, Aurelia, aren't you?" When Mama didn't answer, he turned to me. "She's all right, isn't she?" Before I could say anything, he decided for himself. "Yes, she seems fine." He put his hat on and yanked down the brim. "Good. If everything is under control, I need to get back to work."

I followed him out the door, closing it behind me. "But Papa, I think Mama has a powerful need to see Grandma. She's so lonesome for home."

Papa turned suddenly. "This *is* home, Mem. And your mama will be fine. You'll see to that."

"Yes, Papa, but if we can't have Grandma come, maybe we should have Mrs. Pierce check on Mama to see about her spells."

"Spells?" Papa bit off a hunk of bread. He had to pull hard with his teeth, because the bread had gone stale from being left uncovered. He looked at me for a minute while he chewed and swallowed. "Your mama herself said whatever spell she had is over and done with. There's no need to bring outsiders into our business."

"Yes, Papa, but . . ."

He shoved the rest of the bread into his pocket. "We don't want folks thinking your mama is . . . well, they just don't need to know anything about her. She'll be fine. She *is* fine, and that's the end of it." I watched him stride back to the field, his back stiff. He had planting on his mind. And he'd made it right clear that Mama was to be my problem.

Five

I stayed close by Mama's side for the next few days, watching her face to see if she got that far-off look in her eyes. The weather warmed considerable toward the end of the week, and as the temperature went up, Mama's spirits rose with it. By Friday, Mama seemed well enough to be left alone, and Papa said I could go to school.

I started out that morning, but school wasn't where I was going. I had a plan. I'd been keeping aside an egg a day from our hens all week. Now I packed them in my lunch pail with straw to keep them from getting broken. Even though I was almost sure to get into trouble, I knew what I had to do.

My bare feet hadn't had a chance to harden up much, so I felt every pebble and tree root in the road, but it was good to be free of the cabin again. I pretended I was back in Connecticut, walking into town to see Grandma.

Of course the road didn't look anything like the way to Grandma's. There I'd pass farm after farm, with cows, sheep, and horses grazing in the pastures and wide fields of corn and wheat backing up to the hills. Here there was nothing to see but the infernal trees crowding in on each side.

I went through the long stretch where the trees blocked out the sun altogether. Then I smelled a wood fire and saw a small cabin tucked back in a clearing. Soon I passed several more clearings, and finally I could see the crossroads of Williamson up ahead. There wasn't much to the town, just the big tavern that held the post office and two small hotels, the schoolhouse, a blacksmith shop, and a few houses. Except for one frame house, the rest were all made of logs.

When I went into the tavern, I couldn't see for a minute because the sun had been so bright outside. A man's voice came from the darkness. "May I help you with something, young lady? I'm Major Ballard, the postmaster, storekeeper, and bartender. I assume it isn't the latter you're after."

When my eyes adjusted to the light, I saw him standing behind the counter in the back. I placed my lunch pail on the counter and lifted the straw. "I'd like to make a trade. I have eggs."

Major Ballard raised a huge bowlful of eggs from under the counter. "So do I. More than I could sell in a month. The hens are the only things producing this spring. Eggs are all anybody has for payment. Now if you had some corn seed you wanted to part with, I could trade you plenty for that."

"No, I don't have seeds, but these eggs are special. The hens are . . . the hens are . . . from Connecticut!"

Major Ballard's smile gathered up the skin around his eyes like the pleating around the neck of Mama's good dress. "I'm sure Connecticut hens lay mighty fancy eggs, but I couldn't take on any more eggs if the hens came from Paree, France. Just don't need them and don't want them. Bad enough I have to take eggs from my regular customers. Don't seem to recognize you, though. Whereabouts do you live?"

"Down the road toward Pultneyville. We only moved here last summer."

Major Ballard stroked his beard. "I'd wager I know your plot of land. Put up a log cabin last summer. I think I heard your ma just had a new baby."

"How did you know that?" I asked.

Major Ballard smiled. "Well, if there's any news to be told in these parts, I'm usually the one that hears it, both from the people getting their mail and the post rider with news from south of here. Your pa comes in here about once a week for his mail. He was telling folks that the babe was born right in the middle of the blizzard. Must have been a bit of a fright for your poor mother. How are she and the babe faring now?"

"They're fine," I said. There was no sense in spreading

our troubles to someone who couldn't help, especially if
he might tell others. Should I ask the major not to mention my visit to Papa, or would that only call attention to
the fact that I was doing something I shouldn't? My mind
was racing, trying to keep my plan from falling apart.
"Could I work for the money?" I asked. "I can do just
about anything. I'm strong."

Major Ballard pulled out his ledger book. "Now that I
know who you are, I can just put whatever you need on
your father's account."

"No!" I said, too quickly.

He peered over his glasses at me and raised his
eyebrows.

"It's a surprise . . . for Papa. He might guess if he saw
what I charged."

Major Ballard smiled and drummed his fingers on the
counter. "Suppose you tell me what it is you need, then
we'll figure out how you can pay for it."

"I need paper, an envelope, and the postage. I need to
send a letter right away."

"To Connecticut?"

"Yes!" I said. I almost asked how he knew, but stopped
myself just in time to avoid appearing foolish.

Major Ballard walked over to the big roll of wrapping
paper, ripped off a piece nice and even with the roller
blade, then tore it in half. The one half he folded into the
shape of an envelope. "This take care of your needs?"

"That's perfect. How much does it cost?"

"Well, seeing it's only wrapping paper, there's no charge." He reached into my lunch pail. "As for the postage, I'll take me a couple of these eggs for my own breakfast. I've heard those Connecticut hens lay a mighty special egg."

"Thank you!" I said.

"The post rider's due in right soon. He's already later than usual. You'd best get your letter written so I can send it out with him. He won't be back through here until next Tuesday. You got pen and ink with you?"

I shook my head. What was the matter with me? I'd never given a thought about what I'd use to write the letter.

"Here," Major Ballard said, clearing a space for his pen and inkwell at the end of the counter. "You can use these, but if someone comes in to charge something, I'll have to use the pen to record it in my ledger book."

"Thank you," I whispered, embarrassed to seem so stupid.

The bell over the door jangled and a woman walked in. She was about Grandma's age, dressed all in black with a black bonnet. The way her mouth was pinched up under her long pointed nose, she looked for all the world like a crow. She marched over to us, frowning. "Has the post rider been through yet, Major Ballard?"

"No, Mrs. Foster. He's running late."

The woman pulled an envelope out of her purse and placed a coin on the counter. "Good. I wrote a letter to my sister this morning. I wanted to tell her about our strange blizzard."

Major Ballard shook his head. "She probably won't be surprised, Mrs. Foster. The post rider said he heard it had snowed all over the northern part of New England. Some folks had it much worse than us."

Mrs. Foster clutched at the neck of her dress. "Good heavens! I knew the storm had evil portent. It must be the Lord's vengeance. He's punishing us for our sins."

Major Ballard chuckled. "Now, Mrs. Foster, you don't look to me like a woman who's accustomed to sinning."

Mrs. Foster's eyes stopped his laughter as surely as if she'd hit him with an arrow. "I feel like a sinner every time I have to come into this heathen tavern to send a letter or pick up my mail."

"Long as you're not drinking, you're coming into the post office, not the tavern, ma'am. I'm sure the good Lord can appreciate the difference."

Mrs. Foster pulled herself up taller and glared at the row of bottles behind the bar. "As long as there are sinners in this world, we'll all be punished for it. If you were a godly man, Major Ballard, you'd take those wicked bottles and pour them into the creek."

Major Ballard laughed again. "Now wouldn't that make for a bunch of happy fish. They'd probably be so liquored up, they'd jump right into my frying pan."

Mrs. Foster tossed her head and whirled around so fast, she almost lost her balance as she flounced out the door.

Major Ballard stamped her letter and put it with the rest of the mail. "That's the first I've seen of her in a week. Usually she's in here every day, eavesdropping on everybody else's business instead of tending to her own. Mind my words, she'll be back before you leave. She had a shopping list in her hand and didn't ask for one item on it." He reached out. "Got your letter ready yet?"

"No, sir." I didn't tell him I hadn't even started.

"Seems there's someone else here who needs to tend to her own business." Major Ballard winked at me.

I could feel my face getting red as I dipped the pen in the inkwell. First I addressed the envelope in my best handwriting, in case Major Ballard was judging me by my penmanship. Then I tried to straighten out all the thoughts and concerns that whirled through my head.

Dear Grandma,

I hope this letter finds you in good health. How is the weather there? We have had uncommon bad weather here. Mama was delivered of a babe Thursday last. We were wondering if you could come for a visit. Please let us know.

Your loving granddaughter,
Remembrance Nye

I stared at what I had written. It wasn't at all what I wanted to say. It was as if all the feeling and fear had been squeezed out of the words and they lay on the paper dry as dust. How would Grandma know what I meant? How would she know how much I needed her? How did people learn to use the right words so that their writing said what was in their hearts?

Major Ballard looked over my shoulder. "Finished? I think I hear the post rider."

"Almost." I dipped the pen one more time and scrawled across the bottom, *Mama is having spells. We need you something terrible.* I pressed on the pen so hard, it made a great splotch at the end. The paper looked awful, but I felt better because those words said more than the whole letter. I blotted it, folded it, and put it in the envelope. Major Ballard lit a sealing wax candle to fasten it just as we heard horse's hooves stopping outside.

As soon as I saw my letter safely inside the post rider's bag, I thanked the major and left. I didn't relish being around when Mrs. Foster returned with her shopping list.

At first I thought about going to school. But surely I would be taunted for my tardiness. And I was too excited about mailing the letter to keep my mind on lessons. I'd come back tomorrow and make a fresh start.

As I headed for home, my heart felt heavy and light at the same time. I started talking to myself. That's what I had done when I'd been separated from my family on our journey from Connecticut. Hearing my thoughts out loud made it easier for me to figure things out. I argued the facts of the matter as if I were two separate people.

"You did the right thing, sending the letter. If there's something wrong with Mama, you can't take care of her and the baby, especially if Papa doesn't see the problem. You need Grandma to help."

"But what if Mama's spells were nothing? What if she never has another spell? Papa will be angry that you brought Grandma here for no reason, especially after he said not to."

"So all the better if Mama's fine. Then she'll have a wonderful visit with Grandma."

"And then she'll be all sad again when Grandma leaves to go back home. She'll be more homesick than ever. You're only making it worse. Papa will be angry with you."

"Papa will be angry with me no matter what happens."

I knew the truth of those words the minute they were out of my mouth. It's a good thing I stopped babbling to myself, because I might have missed the sound of the wagon that was coming from Williamson, gaining on me fast. When I stepped off the road to let it pass, I saw that it was the woman I'd seen in the post office, Mrs. Foster. I couldn't tell if she'd seen me or not. She stared straight ahead as she cracked the whip to make her horse go faster. What with all the stumps and underbrush in the road, it seemed a wonder she didn't upset the wagon.

I hadn't gone much farther when I saw the figure of a man walking toward me in the distance, from the direction of home this time. His hat was pulled low over his eyes, so I couldn't make out who it was. I remembered the awful turkey drovers we'd met on our journey to New York. This man was alone, probably just another settler like Papa, but the drovers had left me with a fear of strangers, especially men. Just to be safe, I crouched behind a tree, covered my face with my hands, and waited for him to pass. I listened to his heavy footsteps and didn't get back on the road until I knew he was well beyond me.

I finally reached the turnoff to our house and ran through the woods. If Mama wondered why I was home in the morning, I could just say the teacher had dismissed us early. Mama would believe that, because the last teacher had dismissed class for the slightest reason. An invitation for a quilting bee or a cup of tea could prompt her to send us home after only a half day of learning.

It wasn't until I had started to push open the door that I saw the strange wagon with a horse tied to the big tree next to the cabin. Sure enough, I saw a black-clothed figure sitting across the table from Mama. Joshua was pouting on his bed and didn't jump up when I came in, so I figured Mama must have ordered him to stay put while she had company.

Mama looked up, smiling. She had her good tea set on the table and there was a plate of cookies.

"Mem, come in and meet our guest. She's brought a fine confection to celebrate the birth of the babe."

As I approached the table, the woman turned and I

could see the familiar crow's beak under the brim of her bonnet.

"Mrs. Foster," Mama said, "I'd like you to meet my daughter Remembrance."

"How do you do," I said, ducking my head so she wouldn't see my face. Joshua took advantage of all the attention being on me to make a silent dash for the cookies. He managed to grab one in each hand and slip back into his place without being noticed.

Mrs. Foster squinted, her dark little crow's eyes studying me for a minute. I held my breath. Surely she must recognize me. We hadn't been an arm's length away from each other in the tavern. "A healthy-looking child," she said. "Must be a big help to you. I miss having daughters to work around my house. Mine have all married and moved away. Would you consider hiring her out? I can pay well."

I felt like a farm animal up for barter.

Mama's hands fluttered nervously over the teapot. "Oh, I don't think we could spare her."

"Well, if she has time to go running off, she mustn't be doing much for you."

"I wasn't running off. I had to go to school," I said, hoping to confuse Mrs. Foster.

"Oh, is that where she was?" Mrs. Foster's eyes held mine for a second before I broke away. "Seems foolish for a girl your age to still be in school. What are you, girl? Eleven? Twelve?"

"Twelve," I said. "And I need to go to school, because I'm going to be a teacher."

Mrs. Foster laughed—a dry raspy sound that ended in a fit of coughing. When she recovered, she rose from the table. "I'd best be getting on. Keep my offer in mind. What did you say your name was?"

"Remembrance," I said.

She pursed her lips and studied me again. "You remind me of someone, Remembrance Nye. Can't think who, but it'll come to me. It always does."

Lily started crying right then, so it gave me an excuse to get away from Mrs. Foster. I just wanted her to leave before she remembered where she saw me.

I brushed the telltale cookie crumbs from Joshua's shirt as I passed him, then busied myself with Lily in the far corner of the cabin. After making arrangements for another visit with Mama, Mrs. Foster finally left, and I felt relief flood over me.

I helped Mama with housework all afternoon, just to make sure she wouldn't want to hire me out to the old crow. Mama was so excited to have a visitor, she didn't think to question why I got home early from school. I silently vowed never to do anything behind Mama's or Papa's back again. I'd been lucky this time, but I wouldn't take another chance.

Later that afternoon, Papa came home and pushed the door open so hard, it slammed against the wall and knocked a clay dish off the shelf. "How was school today, Mem?"

"Fine, Papa," I mumbled.

"Speak up, Mem. What did you learn in school today?" His face looked like a thundercloud.

"I can't remember. Nothing in particular."

"That's not the way I heard it. I heard you practiced your penmanship." He tossed a letter on the table. At first I thought it was mine, but then I saw that it was addressed to Papa from someone in Connecticut. It must have come in with the post rider or Major Ballard would have given it to me when I was there. Papa was the man I saw on the road.

And now Papa knew about my letter to Grandma.

Six

Papa made me tell him what was in the letter. I didn't mention the part about Mama's spells, because I couldn't bring myself to say that in front of her. I just told him that I had invited Grandma to come visit.

"Against my direct orders, you wrote that letter?"

"I did, Papa, because I think a visit from Grandma is just what Mama needs to make her feel better."

"You're not to decide what's best for your mother. She'll be fine without any visitors. You're making a big commotion over nothing."

"I think you're wrong, Papa. I think . . ."

"You've done enough thinking for one day!"

"But don't you see that—"

Papa's hand shot out so fast, I didn't see it coming, didn't have a chance to duck. He slapped me hard on the side of the face, the force of it knocking me to the floor. I didn't expect it, because Papa had never struck me before. He'd threatened a few times, but he'd never done it. As I sprawled across the dirt floor, I felt my whole world coming apart.

The shock of Papa's action seemed to bring Mama back to being herself. She was beside me in an instant, helping me to my feet. "Jeremiah, I'll not have you punishing the child for doing something you should have had the sense to do yourself."

"When a man gives an order in his own home, it should be obeyed." Papa lifted his hand again, but Mama stared him down. "Would you strike your own wife now, because you can't admit you're wrong?"

Papa lowered his hand but didn't say anything. Mama hugged me close to her, and Joshua clung to my skirt on the other side. "I'm glad Mem sent the letter," Mama said. "Just the thought of seeing my mother again puts me in better spirits."

Papa opened the door and turned to point a trembling finger at Mama. "I'm going to ignore what you just said to me, Aurelia, because I know you're not quite back to normal yet. But I'll not have you or the children disobeying me. A man has to have control in his own home." He looked at his hand for a moment, as if it belonged to someone else, then he let it drop to his side. He slammed the door as he went out, sending another dish flying from the shelf. It was lucky we only had a dirt floor or we'd be running out of plates.

Mama dipped a cloth in cold water, wrung it out, and pressed it to my cheek. My face stung not only from the pain of the blow, but also from the shame of having disobeyed Papa. This must have been far worse, in Papa's eyes, than anything I'd ever done before. But still, I didn't deserve to be struck for doing what I knew was right.

"It's not like your father to do such a thing," Mama said. "You know, a lot of men beat their wives and children regular, but Jeremiah's a gentle man for the most part."

"I know, Mama."

She wiped my tears with the wet cloth, then tossed it on the edge of the water pail and went to the window, folding her arms tight around herself. "It's this place that's done it to him, you know. This infernal wilderness has a way of creeping inside you and twisting until you hardly know who you are anymore."

Mama was getting that faraway look in her eyes again, and I had the feeling she was talking more about herself than Papa.

"Don't worry, Mama. I'm not hurt," I said, trying to keep her with us. "I shouldn't have gone against Papa's orders, and I shouldn't have lied about going to school. But I'm fine. Really, I am."

Mama turned toward me with the look of a frightened deer. "Lying is a sin. You mustn't sin anymore, Mem. We must all be careful to live according to God's word. The storm, the cold weather, it's because of our sins."

"Mama, I don't think the weather has anything to do with sinning."

"What do you know of it? You're only a child, a willful one at that." Her eyes were shooting sparks now. "Mrs. Foster opened my mind to the truth. It all makes sense. If we don't obey God's will, even in the smallest things we do, God will bring his anger down upon us. He already has."

It seemed that Mrs. Foster had filled the need that Mama had for church, but the things she told Mama only upset her. I'd have to find out when the circuit rider was coming through next. Maybe going to a meeting would help to calm Mama, even if it was in a cabin instead of a church. "Don't listen to Mrs. Foster, Mama. She's just an old busybody."

"I'll not have you speaking of my friend in that way." Mama drew herself up taller and jutted out her chin, the way she did when she stood up to Papa. "Not one other woman in these parts cared enough to come visit me after the birth of the babe."

"Maybe it's not the way things are done here," I said.

Mama glared at me. "It's the custom with civilized people, no matter where they are." She moved to the table, her back to me. When she turned around, she was smiling. "She brought cookies, Mem, and we had a proper tea with my good china and my best linen napkins." She picked up a napkin and smoothed it over the front of her dress, then held it to her as she started to dance around the cabin, slowly at first. "You should have seen Jeremiah Nye when I first met him. It was the Twelfth Night Ball at the town hall. I was only seventeen."

She moved faster now, clasping one corner of the napkin to her waist and stretching the opposite corner out to the side like the full skirt of a ball gown. Joshua giggled and ran over to frolic with her, but she almost stepped on him, as if she couldn't even see him. "Jeremiah was new in town, and every girl had set her cap for him. But I was the one he wanted."

Mama moved in a big circle, nodding and smiling to invisible people. Her happiness filled the cabin so that I could almost see them myself, but I knew the joy was only in her mind, not her heart. Joshua sensed it, too, because he came back to hide behind my skirts, peeking out at Mama as she twirled by.

Mama's moods were changing as fast as the spring storms that moved across our valley in Connecticut. The dark clouds would just barely make it up over Cooper's Hill before they dropped their burden of rain on us, all in a rush. Then it would be bright sun and the fields hot with steam, but you knew there could be more dark clouds hiding over the next valley.

Mama's dark cloud came on just as sudden. She dropped to the floor and curled all up on herself, the way a cat sleeps when the weather is cold.

"Mama? Are you all right?"

She didn't move, her face hidden in the curve of her arm.

"Mama?" When I knelt down and pulled her arm away from her face, I found her staring at the ceiling. "Mama! Don't leave us again, Mama."

I felt Joshua's weight on my back as he leaned in to see. "What's the matter with Mama?" he whispered, with the little click in his throat that told me he was frightened.

"She'll be all right, Joshua." His breath felt hot on my ear and I could smell sugar cookies. If it was my lot to care for Mama and Lily until Grandma came, I'd need to teach Joshua how to help. I turned and held him by the shoulders. With me kneeling, our eyes met at the same level. "You're five years old, Joshua, and getting to be a big boy now. You can help me make Mama feel better."

"Me? How?" He drew himself up taller, pleased.

"See that cloth on the pail? The one Mama used on my face?"

"I see it."

"Dip it in the cold water, wring it out, and bring it back here."

"What's 'wring it out'?"

At Joshua's age, I was doing dishes by myself and had been cleaning the table since age three. Mama babied Joshua, thinking him too young to do the work. When I had complained once to Mama, she had said she'd lost two babies after me and wanted to make sure this son lived to an old age. At this rate, Joshua would live to be a hundred. "Wring means to squeeze the water out of it, Joshua. So it isn't all drippy."

Joshua ran for the cloth, dipped and squeezed it, and ran back with it all drippy.

"Like this," I said. "Twist it." I wrung the cloth, letting the water make a muddy puddle on the dirt floor.

"You said squeeze, not twist."

I tried not to lose my patience with him. "Yes," I said evenly, "I said squeeze, but twist would have been a better word. Now fold the cloth and put it on Mama's forehead."

Joshua bunched the cloth in his hands.

"No, *fold* it."

Joshua looked up, frowning. "I don't know how."

It would have been so much easier to do this myself, but Joshua had to learn. "All right, then. Put the cloth on Mama's forehead and call her name."

"Is she asleep?"

"Not exactly. Just do it. Talk sweet to her."

"Nice Mama. Wake up." He looked at me. "Can I say 'wake up' if she's not asleep?"

"Yes. Now put the cloth on her forehead. Right here."

As soon as the cold cloth touched her skin, Mama's eyes blinked. She looked frightened and confused.

"Tell her everything is all right," I whispered in Joshua's ear. "Tell her not to be afraid."

"Everything is all right, Mama," Joshua parroted. "Not to be afraid." He patted her cheek with his little hand, then leaned down and gave her a kiss. "Are you feeling better, Mama?"

I stepped behind Joshua, out of Mama's line of sight. "That's good," I whispered. "Ask her if she wants anything. A pillow or a cup full of water, maybe."

"Do you want a pillow full of water, Mama?"

Mama smiled and raised up on her elbows. "Now why would I want a pillow full of water?"

Joshua shook his head and giggled. "I meant a cup full of water."

"That would be nice," she said, tousling his hair.

I had moved farther away, near the door. Joshua ran over to the cupboard but couldn't reach the cups. I motioned for him to get the stool to climb on. When he filled the cup, he left a zigzag trail of water all the way back to Mama. I had to stop myself from running over to steady his hand. Mama took the cup and hugged Joshua with her free arm. I slipped outside the cabin where I could watch but not hear their conversation. Mama and Joshua talked for a few minutes, then Lily started to cry and I saw him help Mama to her feet. I watched as Mama picked Lily up, took her to the bed, and started nursing her. Joshua saw me through the door and ran out to me. "I made Mama all better, Mem."

I hugged him and kissed the top of his head. "You did just fine, but now you must stay with Mama and be her helper while I take a walk. Can you do that?"

"Of course I can. I'm big now. Soon I'll help Papa with the plowing like you." He ran back into the house.

I almost looked forward to the time when Joshua would be Papa's helper instead of me. I hadn't seen it happening, but Papa wasn't the same as he had been in Connecticut. He barely smiled and was much quicker to lose his temper.

Now it was even more important for me to devote my time to my studies and concentrate on being a teacher so that I could be ready to go out on my own. Hannah had told me they once had a teacher who was only six-teen years old for the summer session because they couldn't find anyone else to do it. The older boys had finally plagued her enough to drive her away, but that wouldn't happen to me. I'd outwit the stupid lunks and make them look foolish in front of the whole class. They'd not get the best of me.

As soon as I had a chance, I was going to teach Joshua how to care for Lily. In case Mama neglected her, Joshua would need to be able to comfort her and change her. And he'd have to learn how to tell when things were bad enough to run to Papa for help. It would be at least a fortnight before Grandma could get here, maybe as long as a month, depending on how long it took for the letter to reach her. I didn't intend to stay out of school all that time and lose most of the summer session. Besides, I missed Hannah. What good was it to have a best friend if you never got to see her? Joshua would have to do a great deal of growing up in a hurry.

I had been walking along looking at my feet, so it surprised me when I came upon Papa. He was sitting on a stump at the edge of the cornfield, his head in his hands. I froze, not knowing if he had seen me or not. He didn't move, so I took a step backward to get away, and a stick broke with a sharp crack under my foot. Papa looked up and held out his hand to me. I could feel my face crumpling with tears as I went to him. "I'm sorry, Papa. I won't lie to you again."

Papa hugged me and pulled me up on his knee, something he hadn't done since I was Joshua's age. "You're not the only one with regrets, Mem. I never thought I'd turn into the kind of father who knocks his child to the floor."

I started crying hard then, and it wasn't until Papa wiped his eyes that I realized he might have been crying, too. I pulled away and went to sit on a nearby log to give him time to regain his composure. He was silent for a long time. "You were right to send the letter," he said finally. "Aurelia needs to be with her mother until she's back on her feet again. She's too tender for this rugged place. It's like trying to plant a seedling on the windy side of a mountain. She can't put down roots. She was coming along pretty well, though, until the babe was born."

"It's not Lily's fault," I said.

Papa looked puzzled. "Who's Lily?"

"The baby. I named her myself. She can't go through life being called 'the babe.' "

Papa laughed. "You do take charge of things, don't you? Does your mother approve of the name?"

"I don't know. I haven't told her yet."

Papa's face grew serious. "There's a reason not to name a babe this soon, Mem. Many don't survive the first year. You know that."

"Maybe that's because they have no names and think they're not welcome here. They give up and go back to heaven."

Papa ignored my comment. "Your mama does seem to be getting better this week, don't you think? I know she had that one spell, but she's acting more like herself now that the weather's warmed up."

I didn't say anything. The letter to Grandma was already on its way, and Papa had agreed that it was a good idea to have her come. If I told Papa about the spell Mama had today, he might think I should stay home instead of going to school. I knew I could teach Joshua to handle things, but I was pretty sure Papa wouldn't see it that way. Was holding back a truth the same as telling a lie?

I told myself it wasn't.

Seven

I cared for Lily myself most of the weekend, taking her to Mama only when she needed to be nursed. I kept Joshua with me the whole time, showing him everything I knew about infant care, which wasn't a great deal. The weather was warm and sunny, so we could take Lily outside. Mama was in better spirits, even baking some Indian bread. She carved off thick slices while it was still hot from the Dutch oven. "You and Joshua can have some bread, Mem. I'm feeling strong enough to carry Papa's lunch to him in the field, if you'll mind the babe."

"I will, Mama. Take your time and enjoy the fine weather."

Mama put some bread and a hunk of cheese in a basket and covered it with a cloth. She turned at the door and smiled at me. "You've become a great help to me, Mem—a help and a comfort."

"Thank you, Mama." I remembered Grandma's last words to me when we left Connecticut. "Be a comfort to your mama, Remembrance," she had said. It's a good thing I hadn't known then how much comforting Mama would be needing.

Mama was barely out of the door when Joshua ran over to the table. "I want my Indian bread!"

"In a minute, Joshua. First I want to teach you how to change Lily's clouts."

Joshua wrinkled his nose. "I don't want to. Mama does that."

"I know she does, but we talked about this. If Mama has one of her spells, she may not take proper care of Lily. Remember the day I came home from school and found Lily crying and you didn't know how to make her better?"

Joshua nodded warily.

"Well, she quieted down as soon as I changed her, remember? Sometimes that's all she needs. She just wants to be dry. And if I teach you, you'll be able to help her."

"All right," Joshua said, but I could tell his heart wasn't in it.

"You need to have some warm water and a cloth ready." I showed him how to dip hot water from the kettle over the fire into a washbasin. Then I added cold water from the pail. "You must always add some cold water so you don't scald her. Put your hand in the basin to make sure it isn't too hot."

I laid Lily on the bed and unwound the swaddling cloths. The minute her arms were released, she started waving them around, then kicked when I set her legs free. How would Joshua ever be able to wind them back again? The cloths were meant to make the baby's limbs grow straight. Would Lily's arms and legs grow twisted if her swaddling clothes were disarranged for a few hours? I decided they wouldn't. Not if I had her wrapped carefully when I was home.

"You must be mindful of the pins, Joshua. As you pull them out, you mustn't stick her with them." Joshua concentrated so hard on pulling out the pins, I thought he was going to bite off his tongue. "Now fasten the pins to your sleeve so you don't lose them."

"Ow!" Joshua cried, after pushing the pin straight into his wrist.

"That's what I mean about the pins," I said. "They have to go in sideways, like this, in and out of the cloth like a sewing needle." I slid the pin into his cuff. "Now you need to open the clouts."

Joshua's eyes grew wide as he pulled back the cloth. "Lily doesn't have a . . ."

"Never mind about that, Joshua." I hadn't thought about the fact that it wasn't proper for a boy to look at a baby girl without clothes, but I had no choice in the matter. I needed Joshua's help.

"But did she break it?"

"No, girls are different from boys. Like cows are different from bulls."

"Why?"

"Oh, for heaven's sake, Joshua. We're not getting into this now. Ask Mama about it. No, wait! Don't ask Mama. I'll tell you another time."

A smell reached my nose, and I realized we had more than a wet diaper to deal with. I pulled Lily's bottom up off the bed, lifting her by her feet as I'd seen Mama do. "I'll clean her up. Just take the dirty clout for me."

Joshua scrunched up his face and picked up the corner of the cloth with two fingers. Then the stink reached him, and he dropped it on Mama's quilt, with the soiled side down. That's when I decided that Lily would just have to stay in her wet and dirty clouts until I got home from school each day, no matter how many spells Mama had. Many people changed a baby only once a day anyway, so it should be all right. I just knew I wouldn't want to be stuck in the smelly rags, but there wasn't much I could do about it.

I couldn't wait for Monday morning to arrive so I could go to school. I had planned to get up before dawn, but I was awake so much of the night, the sun was long up before I awoke. The smell of smoke brought me out of sleep. Mama had started the fire for breakfast, and all the smoke that drifted around the cabin found its way through the hole in the floor of my loft. After I had dressed and combed and braided my hair, I hardly had time to eat my bowl of mush.

"I saved a bit of the Indian bread for your lunch, Mem," Mama said, handing me the lunch pail. "Enjoy it. We have precious little cornmeal left, and it will be a long time before the new corn crop comes in."

"I will. Thank you, Mama."

I had barely started down the path when I heard Joshua calling my name. I turned to see him running after me on his short legs. "I can't 'member all the things about Lily, Mem. Tell me again."

"Look, Joshua, Mama seems much better today. I don't think you'll need to take care of Lily, because Mama will do it herself."

"But I want to help," Joshua said, his eyes filling with tears. "The way you taught me."

I sat on the trunk of a fallen tree and pulled him next to me. "I'm sure Mama would appreciate your help, and as long as she's not having one of her spells, she'll be able to answer your questions. You don't have to remember everything. I just wanted you to know how to care for Lily in case Mama couldn't."

"All right, Mem." I pulled Joshua to his feet and gave him a gentle shove toward the cabin. He took a few steps, then turned. "Now that I'm big, when do I start going to school with you?"

"Next year," I said. "When you're six."

"But why can't I go today?"

"Joshua! You've already made me late. I have to leave."

I started running down the path. I planned to show Miss Becher what a good student I was, and I didn't want to spoil it with tardiness. When I didn't see another student all the way down the road to Williamson, I realized I had spent more time with Joshua's questions than I had thought.

Sure enough, there were no other students milling outside the schoolhouse when I got there. That was a sure sign that class had started because the boys always engaged in raillery in the school yard until the teacher rang the bell. I hadn't even heard the bell ring this morning, which meant I was very late.

Miss Becher stopped talking when I came in. "Remembrance, it's good to have you join us again, although I would appreciate punctuality in the future."

"Yes, Miss Becher." My seat next to Hannah was taken by another girl. Hannah glanced over her shoulder at me, then looked away. The only other vacant seat was on a bench in the back next to Leonard Crowell. I stood there, not knowing what to do.

"Please be seated, Remembrance." Miss Becher motioned to the empty spot. I slid onto the bench next to Leonard, trying not to look at him. When Miss Becher's back was turned, Leonard leaned over and grinned in my face, then stuck out his tongue. I returned the favor just as Miss Becher looked my way.

"Remembrance Nye, I expect the girls in this class to act like young ladies."

"What about the boys?" I mumbled. It hadn't been loud enough for Miss Becher to hear, but she shot me a disapproving look. I had been in school only long enough to sit down, and already I was in trouble.

I didn't get to talk to Hannah until recess, but even then I had to go look for her. I was surprised, for I thought she'd be as eager to see me as I was to see her. I finally found her sitting under a tree in the far corner of the school yard, trading some of her lunch with the girl who had taken my classroom seat.

I ran over to them. "Hannah!"

I expected her to jump up and hug me, to ask about Mama and Lily, but she didn't even smile. Instead she rolled her eyes and the new girl giggled.

I reached out my hand to the girl. "We haven't met," I said. "I'm Remembrance Nye."

"I know," said the girl, not offering her hand in return. "I'm Sally." She shared another secret glance with Hannah.

"Hannah, could I talk with you?" I asked, motioning for her to follow me across the school yard. I wanted to get my friend away from this new troublemaker. I wondered what she could have said to make Hannah act like this.

"I don't think your father would approve," Hannah said, and the two of them laughed.

"What does Papa have to do with anything?"

Hannah stood up, her eyes narrowing. She looked more like her nasty sister, Mercy, than herself. "Your papa made it quite clear that he doesn't want my family to have anything to do with your family."

"When did he tell you that?"

Sally had come up behind Hannah and was listening to everything we said. Hannah made no effort to get rid of her. "It was last week. You had been out of school for two days and I was worried. I told Mama, and she decided we should visit to make sure everything was all right. We even brought a cake for your mother."

"But I don't understand. What happened?"

"We ran into your father out on the post road. When we told him we were on the way to your cabin, he said your mother was doing just fine, and we didn't need to visit her again."

Hannah glared at me. I couldn't think of a thing to say.

"We ate the cake ourselves that night," she said. "It was delicious."

"I'm so sorry, Hannah. I didn't know you had come."

I put my hand on her shoulder, but she shrugged it away. "Oh, really? Well, I asked your father if I could come visit you if we stayed outside so we wouldn't bother your mother. He told me you didn't have time for such foolishness."

"Hannah, I . . ."

"I have nothing more to say to you, Remembrance Nye. It was an insult to my mother to turn her away. A midwife should be allowed to check on a woman she has delivered. And as for what your father said about you, if you think I'm nothing more than foolishness, I'll not be your friend anymore."

"But I never said that!"

"It doesn't matter who said it. As Mama says, there are two kinds of people around here. There are those who try to belong and those who stay by themselves. Your papa has decided which kind you'll be."

Miss Becher rang the bell. Hannah grabbed Sally's arm and the two of them ran into the school. I couldn't move. I gasped for breath as if I were drowning. How could Papa send Hannah away and then not even tell me about it? Didn't he know how important her friendship was to me?

I wanted to talk to Hannah, to tell her about Mama's spells. I felt the weight of the whole family's problems on my shoulders, and I needed a friend to share my burden.

"Remembrance," Miss Becher called from the school door. "Are you waiting for a written invitation to join us?"

My first thought was to run for home, but that would only convince Miss Becher that I didn't belong in school. And it would prove to Hannah that I was as much a loner as Papa. I ducked my head and slipped quietly back inside. Leonard made a face at me as I sat down, but I

ignored him. I was watching Hannah and Sally whispering to each other. Every now and then one of them
would sneak a glance at me. I glared back.

I watched Miss Becher carefully that afternoon, the
way she smiled when she stopped to help students. She
had a kind face, as if she really cared that we learned our
lessons well. I'd be like that when I was a teacher. I practiced my kind face, smiling just enough to look inter-
ested, but not enough so as to appear foolish. I was deep
in my teacher reverie when Miss Becher called me to
come sit with Hannah and Sally so she could work on
reading with us. Neither of them offered to move over.

"Could you girls please make room for Remembrance?
We can't leave her standing in the aisle for our les-
son. Sally?"

Sally slid over just enough for me to squeeze on the
end of their bench. I was afraid Miss Becher would call
on me to read first, but she chose Sally instead. Sally
struggled slowly, but she didn't make any mistakes. When
it was Hannah's turn, she read quickly and didn't even
stumble over the longest words. It was something com-
plicated about why the colonists wanted to fight for their
independence from England.

Hearing Hannah's voice made me feel all the worse for
losing her as a friend. I thought back to the first time I
met her at our cabin raising last summer. I remembered
the fun we had together, and how we played a trick on

Mercy and her high-and-mighty friend. I had been sure that Hannah and I would be friends for life.

"Remembrance? Did you hear what I said?" Miss Becher was looking at me, waiting for me to say something. She no longer wore her kind face. Hannah and Sally were struggling not to laugh, and I could feel Sally's elbow pushing me to the end of the bench. I gripped the seat to keep from falling. "Can you tell me what that last sentence meant, Remembrance?"

I had no idea what Hannah had been reading, and it was taking all of my concentration not to fall on the floor. I stared at Miss Becher with my mouth hanging open.

"Never mind," Miss Becher said, pursing her lips. "Maybe you'll pay better attention to what you read yourself. The next paragraph, please?"

Sally handed the book to me. I looked to her for help in where to start reading, but she turned away. Finally Miss Becher pointed out the place and I started, speaking in a whisper, stumbling over every other word. Miss Becher towered over me, her shadow falling on the page. "Speak up, Remembrance. We can't hear you."

If she would only let me read it to myself, then tell her what it was about. I knew I could do that, but reading in front of the whole class frightened me into being a fool. My throat closed up and I couldn't say a word.

Miss Becher took the book from me. "I think we need to find a more appropriate reading group for you,

Remembrance. It's important that you understand the meaning of what you read. Come with me." She led me over to a bench with two girls much younger than me. They were reading baby stories—just four or five words in a sentence. Out of the corner of my eye, I could see Hannah and Sally looking over their shoulders and laughing at me. My face burned with shame. And when it came my turn to read, I could barely see the words through my tears.

Now I had no friend in school at all. I thought about home and hoped that Joshua was managing all right with Mama and Lily. I had to keep everything going smoothly until Grandma got here. She'd know how to help Mama and deal with Papa.

And then I'd just have my own problems to worry about.

❧

For the next two weeks, the days followed one another with the sameness of pearls on a string. The weather had warmed, making the newly planted corn fairly leap out of the fertile soil. Papa had been right about this being better land to farm than our old land. But he had been wrong in the way he treated Hannah and her mother. I wanted to tell him that, but ever since he had struck me, I was wary of challenging him. I had started to say something several times but thought better of it. Sometimes I felt so angry with Papa, I had to leave the cabin so as not to speak and get in trouble again.

Each day I came home from school and held my breath as I approached the cabin, fearing that I'd find Mama staring at nothing with Lily and Joshua wailing at her feet. But Mama seemed to be her old self again, tending to Lily and even humming once in a while as she kneaded bread.

Still, each post day I stopped at the tavern to see if Grandma's letter had come. "It's hard telling how long the post takes from these parts, Mem," Major Ballard said. "Your letter might not have reached Connecticut yet." I tried to be patient, but it wasn't easy. Even though Mama seemed much better, I wouldn't feel completely safe until Grandma came.

I still had no friends in school and kept mostly to myself during recess. I ignored the giggles and looks from Hannah and Sally when I had to read with the younger children. I stammered so over the simplest words, I feared Miss Becher would have me read with even younger pupils, but she just looked at me with pity. My dream of being a teacher seemed to be drifting out of my reach.

I knew Sally and Hannah were still talking about me. It wasn't fair of Hannah not giving me a chance to explain. How could she blame me for something I didn't even know about? I thought that after a few days Hannah would get over being angry so I could reason with her, but she didn't. I knew one thing for sure. There would be no sense trying to talk to Hannah with Sally around. I needed to see Hannah at her house, but Papa would never permit that.

Then I had an unexpected surprise. Papa made an announcement Thursday night. "Mem, I'm taking your mama and the little ones with me to Canandaigua tomorrow for some supplies. I think it will do everybody some good to have a change of scenery. We'll be leaving first thing in the morning, and it will likely be past dark when we get back. You could go with us if you want. I'm leaving it up to you."

I longed to see the city again, and the wonderful general store with the peppermint candy, but this might be my only chance to see Hannah alone. I could follow her home from school and we'd finally have our talk. "If it's all the same to you, Papa, I think I should go to school. I've missed too many days already."

Papa raised his eyebrows and grinned at me. "Now I would have wagered you'd decide the other way. It appears our little girl is getting a good head on her shoulders."

I ducked my head so Papa couldn't see the deceit on my face.

The next morning, we all piled into the wagon and Papa left me off at the crossroads in Williamson. As I watched the wagon roll out of town, I had a moment of wanting to run after them. What if I had given up a chance to go to the city only to have Hannah send me packing? But I knew I had to try to set things straight between us, so I turned toward the school.

I could hardly wait until the end of the school day. When it finally came, I hung back and let the others leave first. Hannah and Sally walked right past me without a word. When I thought they were far enough ahead not to see me, I started out. I didn't know where Sally lived, but I hoped she'd soon turn off to her home. We went all the way through town and Sally was still with Hannah. What if Sally was visiting her today? I could only think of three farms on the way to Hannah's house. We passed the first one, and Sally didn't turn off. Then the two of them got laughing about something and sat down to rest on a fallen log. I had to hide behind a tree, lest they look up and see me.

They finally started off again and passed the second farm, then the third. I stopped. There was no sense in going any farther. I turned to head toward home. I had given up my only chance to go to the city for nothing. Never mind the fact that Papa had no extra money for foolishness like peppermint candy. It would have been nice just to see civilization again.

I went a short way, then looked back to see Hannah walking by herself. What had happened to Sally? I waited for a few seconds to see if she was off to the side of the road for some reason, but I saw only the solitary figure of Hannah going off into the distance. This was my chance.

It didn't take long to solve the mystery of the disappearing Sally. A new road was cut back into the woods, which made sense, since Sally had only recently started at school. Her family must be new settlers to the Genesee Country. The fact that she lived so close to Hannah would explain why their friendship had blossomed so quickly. They must have walked to and from school together every day. And knowing Hannah, I thought they had probably chattered every inch of the way.

I turned off at the road to Hannah's house, but she was no longer in sight. When I entered their clearing, Hannah's mother was washing clothes near the cabin. She stood up and wiped her hands on her apron. "Why, Mem! How nice to see you. Hannah didn't tell me you were coming to visit."

"She didn't know," I said. "I'm so sorry about Papa sending you and Hannah away. I didn't know anything about it until Hannah told me. It was a terrible thing to do and I . . . ."

Mrs. Pierce reached out and put her hand on my shoulder. "It's all right, Mem. No need to carry on so. How are your mother and the new babe? Are they getting on all right?"

I didn't have a chance to answer, because Hannah came running around the corner of the cabin with a basket of eggs. She stopped dead in her tracks when she saw me.

"Look who's come to visit," Mrs. Pierce said. "I'll leave

you two alone while I finish up the washing. Have you
told Mem our news, Hannah?"

"No, Mama." Hannah avoided my eyes, but I followed
her into the cabin. She put the basket on the table, wet a
cloth from the water pail, and sat down to wash the eggs.

I sat across the table from her. "What did your mother
mean by your 'news'?"

"You'll hear soon enough." Hannah rubbed at an egg,
keeping her head down.

"Does Sally know?" I asked.

She glanced up. "What does Sally have to do with
anything?"

"Isn't she your friend now instead of me?"

Hannah shrugged, putting the clean egg into a bowl
and moving on to the next one.

"It's not fair, Hannah. You can't blame me for something my father did."

Hannah worked in silence for a few minutes. When
she looked up, her eyes were filled with tears. "I'm not
angry with you anymore, but it doesn't matter. Nothing
matters."

"Why not?"

Hannah put an egg down so hard it cracked. She carefully turned it in the bowl so the crack didn't show.
"We're leaving and moving farther west. Papa heard that
the harsh weather hasn't hit Ohio this summer, so he
thinks that's a better place to farm."

My heart sank. "How long have you known?"

"Papa told us weeks ago, but we weren't supposed to say anything until he was sure the land was sold. I was going to tell you anyway—the day Mama and I tried to visit. Others are leaving, too—the Porters and the Crandalls. They were all at your cabin raising."

"It's not fair!" I said. "Our parents keep dragging us off to places we don't want to go. I can't wait to grow up and make my own decisions."

Hannah raised her eyebrows. "Unless you plan to grow up to be a man, you won't be doing any more deciding than you are now."

I opened my mouth to argue with Hannah until I realized she spoke the truth.

Eight

On Saturday, June 29, everything changed. I knew something was wrong the minute I awoke. It was so cold in my loft, I could see my breath steaming the air. I quickly pulled on my dress and climbed down the ladder. When I opened the door, the ground was white with frost. I ran all the way to the cornfield, hardly feeling the icy ground on my bare feet. Papa was there already. He stood with his back to me, shoulders slumped. The corn, which was a hand high in the field only yesterday, now lay flat and blackened, as if it had been scorched over by fire. I knew better than to ask Papa if we could save the crop this time. I slipped my hand into his. "What will we do, Papa?" I asked, not daring to look at his face.

I felt him shrug. "There's no time to grow another crop of corn, even if I could find the seed. We might bring a field of wheat to harvest, but only if the weather turns good from now to fall. It's rich land, though. Would have been the best corn I ever grew."

He let go of my hand and started back to the cabin. I had the feeling he'd been talking more to himself than to me.

We'd been inside just long enough for Papa to take off his jacket and tell Mama about the lost crop when there was a frantic pounding at the door. Papa opened it to find a wild-eyed Mrs. Foster. She pushed past Papa into the room. "You all must come with me to the camp meeting."

"Begging your pardon . . . ," Papa started, but Mrs. Foster interrupted, pulling on Mama's arm.

"Remember I told you about the camp meeting, Aurelia? It was supposed to start next week, but now, with last night's message from God, they've decided to begin today. We must all repent to save our souls. Who knows how much time we have left? Bring warm shawls and blankets for the children. The meeting will go on well into the night."

Papa blocked the door. "Now see here, madam. I don't know who you are, but I have no intention of letting you drag my family off to some camp meeting just because you think you have a message from the Lord."

Mrs. Foster pointed a bony finger at Papa. "We've all been given the message, but some are too blind to see. The Lord has smote our crops to the ground. Half the people in Williamson are packing up to go—people who have never been to a camp meeting in their lives. The end is near."

"The end of what?" Papa said.

"You fool!" Mrs. Foster spat out the words. "The world is coming to an end and you stand there like a fence post. I'm trying to save your family."

"You're getting riled up over nothing," Papa said, putting on his jacket. "Bad weather doesn't mean the end of the world. Aurelia, I forbid you and the children to go with this woman. Is that understood? And madam, I'm respectfully asking you to leave my house."

Mrs. Foster pushed Mama back to the wall and whispered in her ear. I crowded in to hear. "Those are the devil's words, Aurelia. You know I speak the truth. I'll leave, but I'm coming back as soon as he's gone. You're my dearest friend, Aurelia. I must save you and the children."

Mrs. Foster swept out of the cabin, leaving Mama clinging to the wall. I wondered how dear a friend she could be if this was only her second visit.

"She said she's coming back, Papa," I said. "Please don't let her."

"I'll make sure she's really gone, Mem. I want you to pull in the latchstring and don't let anybody into this cabin until I get back. I'm going to Williamson to ask around and find out how widespread this weather problem is." Papa glanced at Mama, who had begun to tremble. "Mem, you see that everyone stays calm." With that, he was gone. I ran over and pulled in the latchstring, then went to comfort Mama.

"Don't listen to Mrs. Foster, Mama."

Mama slid down the wall and hugged her knees, burying her face in her skirt. We were losing her again. I went to the door and peeked outside. Mrs. Foster's wagon was just disappearing through the trees with Papa striding after her. Surely there was no way she could come back from Williamson with Papa on the road. We were safe for now. I went back inside and crouched next to Mama. I put my arm around her shoulders. "Everything is going to be all right, Mama. We should hear from Grandma any day now, telling us when she'll arrive."

Mama looked up, her eyes red with tears. "Don't you understand, Mem? The world is coming to an end. The only way we'll ever see your grandma again is if we meet her in heaven. That's why we must repent of our sins." She closed her eyes and prayed silently. I stayed next to her, rubbing her back, while Joshua watched, wide-eyed, from across the room. I knew Mrs. Foster was wrong about the end of the world. Surely God wouldn't punish people who worked so hard as our family just to stay alive. What terrible sins had we committed? When Mama calmed down a bit, I'd try to talk some sense into her.

Suddenly the door flew open and banged against the wall. The latchstring! I'd forgotten to pull it in after I peeked outside.

"Your husband is as foolish as he is wicked, Aurelia,"

Mrs. Foster said. "I went down the post road toward Pultneyville just far enough to be out of sight. I hid the wagon in a clearing and saw him head toward Williamson. Now, there's no time to lose. Get the children into my wagon."

Joshua rushed over and clung to my skirt. "We're not going with you, Mrs. Foster," I said. "Go away and leave us alone. You've upset Mama."

Mrs. Foster's little crow's eyes flashed fire. "*I've* upset your mother? It's the good Lord who has shaken her. He's trying to save her soul, and so am I. I'm the only true friend she has." She pulled Mama to her feet, then snatched Lily from her cradle.

"No!" I screamed. "Leave Lily alone." I ran over and tried to grab her, but Joshua weighted me down and Mrs. Foster held me off with an arm that was surprisingly strong for a woman her age.

"Aurelia, gather the quilts and shawls."

Mama obeyed, moving like a sleepwalker.

I made another lunge for Lily, but Joshua wouldn't let go of my skirts and I tripped, landing hard over the bench. The blow knocked the breath clean out of me.

"The boy!" Mrs. Foster shouted. "Aurelia, get the boy."

Mama lifted Joshua in her free arm and took him and the blankets out the door while I gasped for air. By the time I managed to get outside, they were all in the wagon. Joshua and Lily were screaming. I ran to the wagon and grabbed the sideboard, but Mrs. Foster smacked my hand with the whip handle. "Go away, wicked girl," she shouted. "You can stay with your devil father. You deserve each other."

I couldn't reach Joshua and Lily. They were behind the wagon seat, and I could see that neither one was wrapped properly against the cold. Mrs. Foster cracked her whip and her horse lunged forward. There was only one way I could save my family.

"Wait!" I screamed as they started off. "Take me! I want to repent!"

The wagon stopped. I ran and climbed in next to Joshua. Mrs. Foster turned in her seat, her smile making her face a bit less crowlike. "I'm glad you came to your senses, dear."

I tucked the quilt around Lily and Joshua and wrapped myself in a shawl. I gave Mama her shawl, but she only draped it loosely over her shoulders and it soon slipped down. She was deep in conversation with Mrs. Foster about the end of the world and seemed not to notice anything around her, even the biting wind stirred up by the speed of the wagon.

All along the post road, I watched for Papa. My plan was to call out to him in time for him to turn and grab the horse's bridle. I'd make his job easier by pulling the reins away from Mrs. Foster to slow the horse.

It wasn't long before I saw him walking up ahead. Mrs. Foster was practically preaching a sermon, not even watching the road. I gathered my feet under me, getting ready to make a lunge for the reins. When we were almost to Papa, I jumped up and screamed, "Papa! Stop the horse!" My hand just missed the reins when Mrs. Foster cracked the whip and the horse bolted forward. I was thrown back, bumping my head on the wagon floor. I could see the confused expression on Papa's face as the wagon grazed him, knocking him off-balance. I struggled to the back of the wagon and reached out helplessly. "Papa!" I screamed. "Save us!"

Papa started running after us, but there was no way he could catch up to the wagon on foot. Mrs. Foster pushed the team down the road and through Williamson at a full gallop. It wasn't until we were back into wilderness on the other side of town that she stopped the wagon. Then she turned and pointed her whip handle at me. "Get out!"

"If I go, I take my brother and sister with me," I said.

"So be it. I can't save souls that don't want to be saved."

I gathered Lily in my arms, but Joshua started to cry. "Mama! Aren't you coming home with us?"

That seemed to bring Mama back to her senses for a minute. "We mustn't leave the children. Mem didn't mean to be wicked, did you, Mem?"

I shook my head, stalling for enough time to figure out what to do.

"Ask my forgiveness, then, child." Mrs. Foster's lips set in a tight line.

I wanted to take Joshua and Lily and run, but I knew I

had to get Mama away from her as well. "I'm sorry, Mrs. Foster. Please forgive me."

"You must say that you've been a wicked child and that you repent."

I had to swallow hard to keep down the words that bubbled into my throat. "I've been wicked and I repent," I mumbled.

Mrs. Foster lifted her chin and smiled. "Then you may come with us."

I had no idea where we were going, but the trip seemed to take forever. We finally passed through a town named Lyons, then about a mile down the road we saw people selling cakes and beer. Mrs. Foster turned off the main road at that point and into the woods. Before long, we came to a circular clearing larger than any I'd seen since we'd left Connecticut. On the outside of the circle were wooden cabins, tents, and covered wagons. At one end of the clearing was a large pulpit and next to that, a fenced-in orchestra of several dozen musicians. Split log benches filled the remaining space.

Some people gathered around fires, trying to warm themselves, and others were eating and drinking. Here and there crowds formed around a man preaching or someone singing a psalm. We had no sooner found a spot to settle the wagon on the outside of the circle when four preachers climbed the platform and thirty or forty more musicians filed into the orchestra, carrying their instruments. As much as I didn't want to be here, I was curious as to the sound that could be made by so many musicians. Even in Connecticut, I'd never seen an orchestra this large.

The call of a trumpet drew the crowd to their seats. The men took the right side and Mrs. Foster led us to the left with the rest of the women and children.

The first preacher started with a prayer. Then he began his sermon. "Ladies and gentlemen, dark times are upon us," he shouted.

"Amen" echoed around the circle. I looked over my shoulder. People were still arriving.

"God is punishing us for our sins by taking away the very nourishment that keeps our earthly bodies alive. In a few short months, maybe even sooner . . . half of you . . ." He looked around the circle. The crowd hushed, waiting to hear his next words. "Half of you will be buried in the cold ground." I could hear moans and cries from all around. Somewhere a child was wailing. Joshua burrowed into my side and I held Lily close to keep her warm.

"Look at those around you, the families who have come with you. Which ones will you bury in the coming months? If you came with six, only three will continue to draw breath on this earth. The weakest will be the first to go—the elderly and the children."

"No!" a woman's voice shouted. There was a commotion as another woman seated a few rows in front of us fainted and slipped from the bench.

Mama started crying. I reached over and took her hand. "He's not saying the world will end, Mama. Only that we won't have much food."

"Hush," Mrs. Foster snapped. "Listen to the message."

"While our earthly bodies starve, we must find food for our souls," the preacher shouted. He motioned to the orchestra and they commenced playing a hymn. People stood up and began singing. Mama held her head high as she sang. She smiled, but tears ran down her face. I noticed she'd left her shawl in the wagon and wore only her threadbare linen dress. In Connecticut Mama always wore her good dress with a bonnet and her best shawl to go to church. Now she wasn't even dressed properly for the cold.

After the hymn, another preacher took the pulpit. This one seemed to share Mrs. Foster's belief that the world was ending. He droned on and on about how the world would end in fire and only the chosen ones would be allowed into heaven. He frowned and harrumphed and seemed altogether unpleasant. The thought crossed my mind that if this man and Mrs. Foster were planning on being in heaven, I wasn't so sure I wanted to go there. Then I looked around and saw that there were people in the crowd—families like ours—who looked frightened and confused. Some, mostly men, who stayed on the outskirts of the circle appeared to be scoffing at what was being said, although every now and then, one of them would come forward and take a seat. I didn't believe that the strange weather meant the world was coming to an end, but it frightened me to see grown men and women so taken up with the notion.

The bench grew harder as the afternoon progressed. Then the smell of roasting meat reached us from some of the fires. When I said I was hungry, Mrs. Foster pulled out some stale biscuits and strips of dried beef that were so tough and stringy, it was like chewing leather laces. Since Mama didn't have money to buy food, we had no means to be fussy about what we ate.

When I thought I couldn't bear to listen to another gloomy sermon, I asked Mama if I could go for a walk. She said I must stay put and pay attention to every word. Luckily Joshua needed to find a privy and I got Mama's permission to take him. Actually Mama barely glanced my way when I asked, simply waving me away. I rearranged the shawl around Lily as I picked her up, took Joshua by the hand, and felt free at last.

After our visit to the privy, I didn't want to go back right away. There were things far more interesting to see than what was going on at the pulpit. For one thing, there was a group of women dressed in a manner I had never seen before, with bright-colored frocks cut deep at the neckline and painted lips and cheeks. Some young men were playing cards in the shelter of the woods, apparently trying to get in as much sinning as they could before repenting.

The orchestra struck up another hymn—a lively one

this time. People stood and swayed or clapped in time to the music. All the ruckus woke Lily, who had been sleeping peacefully against my shoulder until that moment. She started to cry, and I jounced her around a bit until I realized she must be hungry. "Come, Joshua. We have to find Mama. Lily needs to eat." Since we had been wandering around, the sun had dipped to the level of the treetops and the shadows stretched long across the clearing.

Joshua climbed up on a tree trunk to see over the crowd. His face was lit pink by the setting sun. "There she is! There's Mama!" He pointed to a long line of people making their way to the pulpit.

"Come forward and be saved!" shouted the latest preacher. "Give up your burden of sins." Sure enough, there was Mama, sobbing, being pushed to the front of the circle by Mrs. Foster.

"Hurry, Joshua. We'll never find her when it gets dark." I grabbed his hand and we elbowed our way through the crowd. Everyone was standing now. The music had risen to a fever pitch that made the whole forest seem to vibrate. People were shouting "Hallelujah" and "Amen" and some were speaking in a language I didn't understand. We finally squeezed to the front of the circle, where people were collapsing on the ground. I couldn't tell if they'd thrown themselves down on purpose or if they had fainted dead away. I stepped over the legs and feet, dragging Joshua along behind. I looked for the blue of Mama's dress or her chestnut hair, but I couldn't find her.

Someone had lit lanterns along the edge of the pulpit, and the shadows from the dancing flames made it appear that the bodies were writhing on the ground like serpents. Suddenly the preacher leaned out over the pulpit and pointed directly at me. "You, girl! Repent of your sins or burn in hell." The orange lantern light lit his face from below, distorting his features and making his bushy eyebrows appear as horns that curled up the sides of his forehead.

I screamed and tightened my hold on Lily and Joshua. "Hurry, Joshua," I yelled. "Run!" I felt him trip, and as I turned to pull him up, I ran into a tall man. He lifted Joshua and grabbed me by the wrist, then started moving through the crowd, dragging me along with him.

"Mama!" I screamed, trying to twist out of his grip. "Mama, where are you?" It was then that I saw her. She stood not two arm's lengths away from us, swaying with the music, smiling peacefully, not hearing my screams. As I looked at Mama's face, I feared that she had gone so far away we'd never get her back.

Nine

I had to stop fighting the man, because I almost lost my grip on Lily. I cradled her close to my chest with my free arm and started screaming, not to Mama this time but to anyone who would hear and rescue us. My screams became part of the music and shouts of "Hallelujah" as the man pulled me away from the crowd's center to the outskirts of the circle, where there were fewer people and less hope of rescue. A man leaning against a covered wagon on the edge of the woods looked up. He took a swig from a clay jug. "Your young'uns don't take much to preachin'?"

"He's not our father," I cried. "Please! Help us!"

"Yes, he is," Joshua said.

I looked up for the first time to see Joshua clinging to Papa's neck.

Papa released his grip on my wrist and I hugged him with a surge of relief. Then he took Lily from my arms. I had been so filled with my own fear, I hadn't realized she was still crying. "How did you get yourselves in this predicament? I told you not to let that woman back into the cabin."

"I'm sorry, Papa. I tried to keep Mama there, but I couldn't. I peeked outside and left the latchstring out by mistake, and Mrs. Foster got in and . . ."

"That makes no matter now. I should have stayed to make sure that woman didn't come back. It wasn't hard to figure out where she was taking you. Where is your mother?"

I searched the moving mass of people near the pulpit and saw her, turning slowly with upraised arms. "There." I pointed.

As soon as Papa saw her, he handed Lily to me without letting his eyes leave Mama, as if he thought she might disappear if he looked away. "Don't move from this spot," he commanded.

I watched as Papa pushed his way through the crowd to Mama, then took her arm to lead her back to us. Mama put up no struggle, but Mrs. Foster was arguing with Papa, and she shouted at him as he took Mama away, shaking her finger at him. When Mama got closer, I could see she had that faraway look in her eyes, only now she was smiling and moving slowly as if in a dream.

"Are you all right, Mama?" I asked.

She looked toward me, her eyes vaguely questioning, but she didn't answer. And she didn't stop smiling.

As we started to drive off, I spotted Mrs. Foster again— saw her beady eyes follow our escape. Her lips were moving, but I couldn't hear her words. From the look on her face, I feared we might not have seen the last of her, no matter what Papa had said to her.

It was slow going on the way home. Lily and Joshua both fell asleep, lulled by the rocking motion of the wagon. Papa had forgotten to bring a lantern, so the oxen had to pick their way along the road by what little moonlight came through the trees. We missed the turnoff to our land altogether and didn't realize it until we came to the town square in Pultneyville. By the time we got home, the sky was beginning to lighten in the east.

Papa built a fire and made coffee and I started heating the griddle for fried mush. Mama seemed capable of little more than nursing Lily, and that only after I had placed the babe in her arms and pleaded with her to feed her poor hungry daughter.

I checked the supply of dried corn and found there was just an inch or two covering the bottom of the barrel. I showed Papa.

"Is this the last of it?" he asked.

I nodded.

"I wish your mother had told me sooner. I'll need to see if someone has corn to spare. I'll have to trade for labor. The little money we have left I was saving for a better plow."

I wondered what good a better plow would do if everything we grew was killed by frost, but I held my tongue. I knew Papa wasn't really talking to me. He was telling me the things he would have told Mama if she were able to listen. But Mama was too far away to care about plows and corn now. I looked over at her. Lily had fallen asleep in her arms, and Mama stared straight ahead, her lips moving. I put Lily in her cradle and left Mama alone while I tended to the chores that needed doing.

I took the last of the corn outside to grind with our mortar and pestle. There was a gristmill in Pultneyville, but we couldn't waste money having our corn ground when we could do it ourselves. Last fall, Hannah's father had shown Papa how to make an Indian mill. They started with a big stump near the cabin and cut a hole in the top with an ax. Then they set a fire in the stump and put in hot stones until it had hollowed out deep enough to be a mortar. They made a hardwood pestle and suspended it from a small sapling next to the trunk. I pulled down on it to mash the dried kernels of corn, bending the sapling. Then when I let go, the sapling sprang upright again, lifting the heavy pestle. It was easy enough work that even Joshua could have done it if he had been tall enough to reach the pestle.

The rhythm of the work soothed me now, giving me time to think. Each thud of the pestle meant that time was passing. Was Grandma even now starting out on her journey to us? Would she come right away, without stopping to send an answer? That thought hadn't occurred to me before, and now I listened for wagon wheels rather than hoping for a letter. Maybe one of my uncles, or probably Grandpa, would bring her directly, since he no longer farmed. My uncles would be busy like Papa with putting in new crops. With each pull on the pestle, I thought of Grandma, willing her to come soon.

I had just ground the last of the corn and gathered every scrap of it into the cornmeal crock when Papa came back—empty-handed.

"Was there no one to sell you corn, Papa?"

Papa shook his head. "Not a soul. Everyone I talked to had used most of their supply to replant. I heard tell that some have bought from the Indians at Irondequoit Bay. Seems they've put aside a good store of grain and are willing to trade for it. I'm going to head out now, while they still have a surplus to trade. Word is getting around fast, and everybody will be going there before long."

"May I go with you, Papa?" I had seen some Oneida Indians from a distance on our journey from Connecticut. I jumped at the chance to meet some of the Indians here up close. According to what I had heard in school, the Irondequoit Bay Indians would be Senecas, for that was their fishing ground.

"You need to take care of your mama and the children,

Mem. I'll have to be gone overnight. No telling what your mama might do if she were left on her own."

I followed Papa into the cabin. "But Mama will be by herself when I'm at school, Papa. Surely she can manage for one night." Even as I said the words, I knew in my heart that Mama shouldn't be left alone.

"I know your schooling means a great deal to you, but you know we can't leave your mother by herself anymore. Maybe if your grandmother comes . . ."

"*When* she comes, Papa."

I watched as Papa took his good shirt and his extra everyday one from the chest of drawers. "You said you'll be gone only one night, Papa. Why do you need so many clothes?"

He folded the shirts and packed them in a burlap sack. "I need them for trade. They told me in Pultneyville, the Indians like shirts and breeches." He pulled out his good pair of pants, looked at them for a moment, then stuffed them into a second sack. "No use for fancy dress anymore," he mumbled.

"Do they want dresses?" I asked. "I don't need my good frock. It's almost outgrown."

"Didn't hear tell of them wanting dresses." He shouldered the two sacks, then stopped at the door. "George Pierce and his family have moved on to Ohio. Left this morning. You and their girl were friends, weren't you?"

I had held a small hope that Hannah's father might

change his mind about moving, but now I'd never see her again. People slipped through my fingers like water. "Of course we were friends," I said. How could Papa even ask me that? Didn't he know how much my friendship with Hannah had meant to me? "She was my best friend before you told her not to come here anymore." There. I'd finally said it.

Papa looked puzzled at first, then I could see his eyes change as he remembered. "I didn't want her mother spreading tales about your mama."

"Why would she do that?"

"Everyone knows midwives gossip. They sit around with all the women, waiting for the birth of a babe, and before you know it, they've learned everything about your family. And as if that wasn't enough, they go and spread your family secrets all over the countryside."

"But she wouldn't have done that," I said.

"No sense in taking the chance." With that Papa left. I was still angry for what he had done, but it didn't change the fact that Hannah would have moved away even if we had been friends all along.

Mama and Joshua soon fell asleep, and I could hardly keep my own eyes open. I decided to nap outside the cabin so I'd wake up if anyone, especially Mrs. Foster, approached. I leaned against the maple tree, pulled my shawl around me, and kept my hand on a large club of a limb for protection. It wasn't long before the sound of horse's hooves interrupted my sleep, but it wasn't Mrs.

Foster. It was some man I didn't know. He was tall and gray haired with a well-trimmed beard.

He dismounted and tossed the reins over a low-hanging tree limb. "I have business to discuss with your father. Could you fetch him for me?"

I stood up, hiding the club behind my skirts. I'd learned to trust no one. "He's not here right now."

"Then when will he be back? The business is of some urgency."

I didn't want to let this man know that we'd be unprotected overnight. "He'll be along later—much later. Too long for you to wait for him."

"Very well. Then tell him that Silas Turner of the school board was here. Since the Pierces left this morning, we need a place to board the schoolteacher. Yours is the only family who hasn't put up the teacher yet, so it falls to you. I'll be bringing her over tomorrow after school, though I had hoped to get her settled in tonight."

I thought of Papa and how he wanted to keep Mama's condition secret to all but family. "I don't think my father will agree to it, sir. We've little space and not much food to share."

Mr. Turner looked at our cabin. "Seems an adequate shelter to me. As for food, you'll receive a small stipend. Enough to purchase what extra you'll need. Besides, this isn't a matter of choice. You attend the school, do you not?"

"I . . . yes, I have, but now I'll not be returning."

Mr. Turner remounted his horse. "That makes no difference. If you've been attending classes, you're obligated to put up the teacher for a spell. You have younger children in the family? A brother about ready to start his schooling, I believe?"

"Yes, but . . ."

Mr. Turner's horse danced a little sidestep, eager to be off. "Tell your father if he wants his son to be educated, he'll board the teacher."

"But could you wait and not bring her right away? Could you wait until you've talked to Papa?"

"I'll talk to him when I bring Miss Becher." Mr. Turner kicked his horse and was gone, leaving me standing with my mouth open. Part of me wanted to sing with joy that Miss Becher would be staying with us—a real teacher to talk to at night. Maybe she'd let me continue my studies with her, and I could prove to her that I was as smart as any of the pupils she had in school.

But another part of me shuddered at what Papa would say when he heard that we had to share our cabin with an outsider—an outsider who would see and know the truth—that Mama was going mad.

Ten

Mama slept the better part of the day and so did Joshua, curled up on the bed beside her. I kept watch outside but dozed off every now and then. That night I made cornmeal mush for dinner and managed to stir it well enough to keep it from sticking to the pot. Maybe there was hope for me as a cook after all. At least I'd know how to make mush, since that and eggs were the only things we had left to cook. Papa had gone deer hunting several times through the winter but hadn't managed to shoot one, and we had long since run out of our meat supply from last summer.

How I regretted not paying more attention to Mama when she had tried to teach me baking skills. Now when I asked her for recipes for corn bread and johnnycakes, I couldn't hold her attention well enough to learn them.

After I cleaned up the dinner dishes, I tried to get Mama to talk to me, but she just sat and mumbled to herself so quietly I couldn't make out the words. Her hair had come partly undone, and wisps of it hung in her face. That wasn't like Mama. She had always spent so much time trying to look her best. And she had taught me to brush my hair a hundred strokes each night.

I got her hairbrush and tried to hand it to her, but she didn't take it. "Wouldn't you like to brush your hair, Mama?"

She finally took the brush, turning it over and over in her hands, as if she didn't know what it was.

"Let me do it for you, Mama." I took the brush and led her over to the stool by the fire.

She didn't seem to know I was near her as I plucked the pins from her hair. I gave her the hand mirror so she could watch what I was doing, but she didn't look at her reflection. It took a long time to undo the braid, as I had to work the hair carefully through my fingers to get the snarls out. Mama's hair, which had once been a wonderful shiny chestnut, now seemed dull and lifeless, like Mama herself.

Once the tangles were gone, I brushed Mama's hair in long strokes. *One . . . two . . . three . . .* I couldn't help thinking that only recently, she had been the one to fuss over my hair, brushing it every night. I remembered how upset she'd been on our journey, when I'd foolishly cut off my braids. She had saved those braids for weeks, and for all I knew, she still had them tucked away someplace. She had always told me that a woman's hair was her glory.

Twenty-five . . . twenty-six . . . twenty-seven . . . "Doesn't that feel better, Mama? I've got out all the tangles now." Her head pulled back with each long stroke, and soon I could hear her humming in rhythm to the brush.

Fifty-seven . . . fifty-eight . . . fifty-nine . . . I began singing along with her, recognizing the tune of an old hymn. Soon Mama started coughing. I feared she had caught cold at the camp meeting. I'd have to make sure she dressed properly for the weather from now on.

Seventy-one . . . seventy-two . . . Mama caught my wrist and pulled me around in front of her. "You mustn't sin anymore, Mem. Will you promise me that?"

"Of course, Mama. Don't worry. Everything will be all right." Mama let go and I started brushing again, forgetting where I had left off.

Eighty-one? . . . eighty-two? . . . eighty-three? I could see myself in the mirror behind Mama, and it surprised me how much I had grown to look like her. She started to rock back and forth on the stool, letting the mirror slide to the floor. I wrapped my arms around her and pulled her back against my stomach, holding tight to stop her rocking. "It's all right, Mama. I'll take care of you." Just as she seemed to relax, we heard a noise outside the cabin. "What was that?" Mama whispered, tensing again.

"Probably just an animal," I said.

Mama jumped up and took Papa's double-barreled shotgun from the wall. "Quick, Mem. Bring a lantern."

"Mama, let's just wait to see if it goes away."

Mama grabbed the lantern herself and went for the door. She had the shotgun balanced on her hip with her finger on the trigger. When she elbowed open the door, we saw a figure in the lantern light.

The gun exploded. The figure fell to the ground. It wasn't an animal. It was a man lying on his stomach. "Mama! What have you done?" I ran outside and crouched next to the man. He had long greasy yellow-white hair sticking out from under his raggedy hat and he wore buckskins.

"Mem, get out of the way." Mama had set down the lantern and was holding the gun in both hands now, aiming directly at us.

The man lifted his head and I recognized him. "Mama, don't shoot! It's Artemus Ware. He's the man who helped me last year when I got separated from you and Papa on our journey."

Mama let the gun barrel drop a bit. That's when Artemus Ware dove for it. The blast went into the ground this time. He took the gun from Mama and tipped his hat. "Beggin' your pardon, ma'am, but you could surely use some lessons in handling firearms. I learned long ago that when a woman takes aim at me, I hit the dirt first and ask questions later."

He carried the shotgun across the yard and wedged it between two tree limbs, high enough that Mama would have a hard time reaching it. "I learned that when Arabella Hotchkiss got it into her head that I'd stolen her cow. I said to her, 'Arabella, the last thing I want to be doin' is dragging an old cow through the wilderness.' "

He was walking back toward Mama now, moving carefully and talking softly. Mama watched him but didn't say anything. Joshua had awakened from all the commotion and was peeking around the doorframe.

"Then," continued Mr. Ware, "Arabella got this notion that I was talking about dragging *her* across the wilderness. 'Call me an old cow, will you, you old goat!' " Mr. Ware made his voice high and warbly for Arabella. "She never gave me a chance to explain. It was just *blam*! Shot a hole clean through my hat. If I'd been an inch taller, I'd be pushin' up daisies."

I ran over to Mr. Ware and hugged him. "I thought I'd never see you again. Remember I told you about him, Mama? He fed me when I was lost and hungry, and he would have stayed with me until we found you and Papa, only he got bit by a rattlesnake." I squeezed his hand. "I was afraid you were dead."

Mama ran her fingers nervously through her hair. "I don't know. I don't . . . know." I could tell she was scared of Mr. Ware, which wasn't surprising, because he was a fearsome-looking man. I had been frightened of him when I first saw him, too. He had coaxed me out of my hiding place with his stories and by the wonderful smell of the rabbit meat he had cooked for me. He had saved my life.

Mr. Ware tipped his battered old hat to Mama. "I was going to wait for morning to call on you. Didn't mean to barge in like this. I'll be on my way, now that I know for sure the young'un is safe."

"Wait! How did you find us?" I asked.

Mr. Ware stopped and brushed off his buckskin breeches, a useless effort because they carried so many layers of dirt, a brushing would do no good at all. "As soon as I recovered from the rattler bite, I set off to inquire after you. I stopped at Belle's Tavern and she said you'd been there, but you'd run off during the night. I worried plenty about you. Looked through the woods in them parts for quite some time, from Belle's Tavern on toward the Genesee Country, but nobody knew what happened to you. Then I was out in Ohio last month and met a man named Nye—I remembered that was your name—and he said he had a cousin who settled somewhere near Williamson."

"That's our cousin Lyman," I said.

Mr. Ware nodded. "I believe that was him. When I heard where you were, I decided to look you up on the way back to New England."

I could see from Mama's eyes that Mr. Ware's mention of New England had caught her interest. "Where in New England is your home, Mr. Ware?"

"Don't have one certain place to call home, Mrs. Nye. I live on my own and travel back and forth through the wilderness. Sometimes I stop and stay with friends."

"You can stay here," I said. "Couldn't he, Mama?"

Mama gathered her apron in her hands and held it tight to her chest. "It wouldn't be proper, Mem. Not without your father here." Then she realized she had given away the fact that we were alone and dropped the apron to press her hands over her mouth.

"I'll be on my way, ma'am. Sorry for the intrusion."

"No, wait!" I said. "Could you stay nearby and come back in the morning?"

Mr. Ware tipped his hat again and smiled. "I'd be honored . . . and I'll bring the breakfast." He disappeared into the darkness.

I felt safe just knowing Mr. Ware was close by. If you met him and Papa for the first time, it would be Papa you'd want to invite into your cabin. You'd probably send Mr. Ware packing, or at the very least, you'd hope that he went away on his own. But I knew that in the wilderness, you couldn't have a better friend than Artemus Ware.

✤

I awoke the next morning to the smell of roasting meat. Joshua followed me out the door. "That's the man who was here last night. Who is he?"

"A friend of mine, Joshua. A good friend."

Mr. Ware had a fire going and was squatting next to it, turning a rabbit on a spit made out of sticks, the same as

I'd seen him do on our journey. Joshua clung to my skirts as we approached him.

Mr. Ware stood up and grinned. "So, who's this?"

"Joshua," I said. "My little brother. He was hiding behind Mama's skirts last night. That's why you didn't see him."

"I was not hiding," Joshua said, frowning.

Mr. Ware bent down and reached out his hand. "Pleased to meet ya, Joshua Nye."

Joshua shook his hand, then scrunched up his nose. "You smell powerful bad."

"Joshua, mind your manners!"

Mr. Ware laughed. "The boy is simply making an observation, Mem. A true one at that." He leaned close to Joshua. "The stink of me keeps the varmints away. I use it as protection."

"Oh." Joshua nodded solemnly. "Good idea."

"Is your mama ready for her breakfast?"

"No," I said. "She's still sleeping." I didn't want to hurt his feelings by telling him that Mama had spent a good part of the night at the window, fretting that he'd come in and kill us all. Nothing I had said could convince her otherwise.

"Well, let's have us our little feast and we'll save some for your mama to eat later."

Mr. Ware cut off hunks of meat for us and we all settled down around the fire. It tasted even better than it smelled. We ate greedily with our fingers and licked the grease from them. "We haven't had meat for a long time," I said. "We haven't had much food at all."

He looked up, surprised. "Oh? Why's that?"

"Well, what with the weather, our crops have been killed. Some say we'll starve before long."

Mr. Ware stood up and held out his arms. "Do you see me growin' any crops? Do I look like I'm starving to death?"

"Well, no, but . . ."

"How in tarnation could you starve? These woods are filled with dinners walking around on four legs. You been waitin' for them to jump into your kettle and cook themselves?"

Joshua laughed so hard at this, he almost choked on the big hunk of rabbit he'd shoved into his mouth.

"Papa isn't very good at hunting," I said. When I saw Mr. Ware's look of disgust, I added, "He had no need to hunt in Connecticut. We raised pigs, calves, and chickens for meat."

Mr. Ware pointed a gnarled finger at me. "If I was you, I'd start depending more on myself and less on the papa that dropped me off the back of a wagon."

"Don't talk about my father like that. You've never even met him. Falling out of the wagon was my fault. Besides, you don't understand everything that's going on here."

Mr. Ware leaned back against a tree and folded his arms. "I understand that you have a papa who's not providing for his family and a mama who don't use the good sense God gave her." Just then Lily started crying in the cabin. Mr. Ware glanced toward the sound. "And a baby brother or sister whose care prob'ly falls mostly to you, I'd guess."

"Well, it may look that way to you, but Mama and Papa mean well."

He picked up a discarded rabbit bone. "Graveyards are filled with people who mean well."

I started to cry, partly from anger at hearing Mr. Ware speak ill of my family but mostly from knowing that he told the truth. He came over and sat down, putting his arm around me. "I don't mean to upset you, girl, but I knew the first time I laid eyes on you that you was stronger than most. If I had a daughter, I'd want her to be like you."

That got me crying even more, and he let me go on for a bit until I settled down. "All right," he said. "Now that you've got the feelin' sorry for yourself out of the way, do you want to learn how to put food on the table for your family?"

"Yes," I said, "I do." And for the first time in a long while, I felt a sense of hope.

Eleven

As Mr. Ware walked along, his eyes searched the ground. "One thing to remember—iffin you want to catch a rabbit, you have to think like a rabbit."

That caught Joshua's attention. "Really? What do rabbits think about?"

"Same thing as any animal thinks about. Food. They'll find the best place to go for food, and they'll leave a trail." He brushed aside some dead leaves to reveal a small pile of rabbit droppings.

Joshua squatted down. "Is that rabbit food?"

Mr. Ware laughed. "No, that's what comes out the other end. It's a sign that rabbits come along this way. Look. There's another pile up ahead. We've found ourselves a rabbit trail. Now we need to put up a blunder snare."

He cut a branch from an evergreen that was full of twigs all around. Then he laid the branch across the path and broke away some lower twigs to make three open-ings just big enough for a rabbit to hop through. He tied a rope noose with a slipknot and fastened it to the branch over one of the holes. "When the rabbit comes hopping through here, his path will be blocked, so he'll have to go through one of those openings I made. We'll have a noose hanging in each one. He'll put his head right through the loop, and the harder he tries to pull away from it, the tighter the rope will get."

"Will it kill him?" I asked.

"Most likely. If it doesn't, you'll have to kill him your-self. And seeing a rabbit struggling in the snare won't stop another rabbit from jumping through the noose right next to it. You might come back and find rabbits in all three snares."

He showed me how to tie the nooses for the other snares and hang them in place.

"How long will it take before we catch a rabbit?" Joshua asked.

"We won't snare any while we're standing here. Come down to the creek and we'll catch a fish while we're waiting."

"We don't have a fishing pole," Joshua said. "Do you have one?"

Mr. Ware smiled. "Don't need one if you're smart. I'll show you how to tickle a trout."

"That's silly," Joshua said, but he walked close to Mr. Ware as we headed for the creek.

As soon as we could hear the water, Mr. Ware shushed us. "Walk quiet, now, so the fish can't feel our footsteps. And make sure your shadow doesn't fall on the water. Here's a good spot."

"What do we do?" I whispered.

"You're going to slip your hands into the water, then pull them back to you, real gentle. If you feel a fish, tickle it along its sides until it's still, then you can lift it and toss it on the bank."

I thought he might be making a joke, but Joshua and I followed him as he lay down on his stomach and eased himself up to the edge of the water. I copied what he was doing, trying to be as quiet as possible, until Joshua made a big splash, sending water over us all.

"Now look what you've done, Joshua," I said. "You've scared all the fish away. This isn't just a silly game. We have to learn how to do this. At least I do."

"I saw a fish, Mem!"

Mr. Ware patted his back. "Well, iffin you did, I'm sure that fish is a long ways off by now. Let's find another good fishing spot." He led us along the creek bank to a place where the gnarled roots of a cedar tree stuck out over the water. He crouched down and looked under the root. "There's a nice one," he whispered.

"A nice what?" Joshua asked, and with a splash, a fish appeared from under the root and swam downstream.

"You have to be very clever, Joshua," Mr. Ware said. "You can't let 'em know you're watching."

We went to yet another spot, and this time, I told Joshua to sit and watch. I slid my hands silently into the water and drew them back to me, watching Mr. Ware to make sure I was doing it right. I did it slowly, over and over, but there was no sign of a fish. Then suddenly I felt one. My heart was beating so hard, I was sure I would scare it away, but I tickled it as gently as I could. Sure enough, the fish grew still under my fingers. I put my hands underneath and tossed it up onto the bank.

"I did it!"

Mr. Ware grinned. "Now that you know what it feels like, you'll be able to bring home some fish every day."

I watched the fish flopping on the bank. It was big enough to make a meal for the whole family. Mr. Ware showed me how to clean the fish, which wasn't pleasant, but I knew I could do it for the sake of a good meal.

"Now let's go back and see if we've had any luck with the snares," Mr. Ware said. "It's probably too soon, but you never know."

As we walked along, I prayed that if we had caught a rabbit, it would be dead. I couldn't bear the thought of killing an animal. We heard the thrashing around before we saw the rabbit. The noose had caught it around the middle of its body rather than its neck, so even though it was tightening the rope with its struggles, the snare couldn't kill it.

As much as I craved rabbit meat, I had the strongest urge to let the poor animal go. Mr. Ware picked up a large rock and handed it to me. "Hold the rabbit, and bring this rock down with all your strength on its head."

I dropped the rock. "I can't. Couldn't I just take it home and have Papa shoot it?"

Mr. Ware folded his arms. "You might as well just let it go, then. No sense trying to teach you anything iffin you're going to go all soft on me like one of them fancied-up city girls."

"That's not fair. I can do it. I've just never killed anything before."

"Then it's high time you started, unless you want to starve to death." He picked up the rock and handed it to me. "Hit it hard the first time so the animal don't suffer."

I dropped to my knees next to the rabbit, held its trembling body down, and closed my eyes, raising the rock over my head.

Mr. Ware grabbed my wrist. "Tarnation, girl. You're like to bash your own hand iffin you don't watch what you're doing."

I took a deep breath and raised the rock again, barely able to see the rabbit through my tears.

Joshua started crying. "Don't hit the rabbit with that rock, Mem. I want to take it home and keep it. I'll feed it."

"Stop it, Joshua! We need the rabbit to feed *us*." With that I brought the rock down hard on the rabbit's head and cringed at the thud.

Mr. Ware examined the rabbit. "Good work, Mem. I couldn't have done better myself. Now I'll show you how to dress it out." He hung the rabbit from a tree and showed me how to gut and skin it. "The rabbit skin can be used for trade if you salt it so it doesn't rot. Or you can make some warm clothes from it."

I only nodded, because I had such a terrible lump in my throat, I couldn't speak. When the grisly job was done, we headed for home. I wasn't sure that rabbit meat would taste good from now on. Tickling a fish out of a stream was one thing, but bashing some poor creature over the head was quite another. Still, I knew I had to do it if we were to survive.

The time had passed so quickly with Mr. Ware, I would have thought it had been an hour at most. But as we walked toward the cabin, I was surprised to see that the sun had risen high in the sky and I felt a rumbling in my stomach that told me it was near the middle of the day.

"Mama must be worried about Joshua and me," I said, walking faster. "I should have told her we were going." The thought occurred to me that it was quite possible Mama hadn't noticed us missing at all if she were in one of her spells. Then another thought hit me—Lily! What if Mama wasn't tending to her? What if she wandered off and left Lily all alone? I had checked on Mama just before we left and found that she and Lily were both sleeping. Still, I should have left Joshua with her. Mama just wasn't reliable anymore. As we neared the cabin, I heard Papa calling me.

"Here I am, Papa. I'm coming!" I ran the last part of the path, with Mr. Ware and Joshua close behind.

When Papa saw us, he picked up his shotgun. "Just stop right where you are, or I'll drop you in your tracks. Mem, Joshua, get over here."

"Thunderation!" Mr. Ware mumbled, raising his hands. "You've got the gun-happiest parents I ever did see. Not a whole brain between 'em."

"Papa, it's all right. Look what I have." As I held out the rabbit, I realized my hands and apron were covered with blood.

Papa kept his eyes on Mr. Ware as he grabbed my arm and pulled me around behind himself. "What did he do to you, Mem?"

"Nothing, Papa. He taught me how to snare a rabbit. It's the rabbit's blood, not mine."

There was no time for more explanations because just then, a wagon came rolling in. It was Mr. Turner with Miss Becher. Mr. Turner reined in his horse and jumped from the wagon. "What in God's name has happened here, Nye?"

Miss Becher stared, openmouthed, from Mr. Ware, to me, to Papa, who was still pointing his gun at Mr. Ware.

"I don't see how any of this is your business, sir, whoever you are," Papa growled.

"I'm Silas Turner from the school board. Didn't your daughter tell you I was coming this afternoon?" He stared at my bloody hands, then at Artemus Ware. "Does this man live here with you? What's happened to the girl?"

"Mr. Turner," Miss Becher called. "Couldn't we leave and come back another time?" She was clutching the sideboard of the wagon so tight, her knuckles looked as if they were carved out of white marble.

"Come back?" Papa said, annoyed. "What for?"

"Miss Becher is the schoolteacher. She'll be boarding with you for the next month."

"Boarding!" Papa practically shouted. "Good Lord, we can't take in a boarder!"

Mr. Turner was already pulling Miss Becher's bags from the wagon. He strode over and deposited them by the cabin door. "I didn't come here to have a discussion about this. It's been decided." He reached in his pocket and handed Papa a small leather pouch. I could hear coins jingling. "This is the stipend for her food."

"Who decided this without my consent?" Papa tried to give back the money, but Mr. Turner was already out of reach. "My wife isn't well," Papa said, helplessly holding out the pouch of coins. "She has all she can manage without adding another person."

Mr. Turner had just helped Miss Becher from the wagon when he stopped and stared in the direction of the cornfield. "Perhaps your wife would be in better health if she dressed more appropriately for the weather."

We all turned to look. Mama was half walking, half dancing down the path from the cornfield. She had Lily on her hip and she wore nothing but her chemise. Her hair flowed loose down her back. "Oh, no, Mama," I breathed. I dashed into the cabin and grabbed the quilt from the bed. I nearly tripped over it three times as I ran to meet Mama. I threw it over her shoulders and pulled it closed across the front to cover her, almost smothering poor Lily. When I looked up, Mr. Turner was making a hasty retreat in his wagon.

As we neared the cabin, Miss Becher stood speechless, unable to take her eyes from Mama. She looked stricken at the prospect of having to live with us.

"We're not accustomed to having visitors," I said, as if that would somehow explain why my mother was running around half naked. Papa took over for me and led Mama into the house.

Miss Becher blushed, suddenly realizing her rudeness in staring at Mama. She shifted her gaze to Mr. Ware, who had just come up beside her.

He tipped his hat and gave her a big toothless grin. "I'd be most honored to share *my* room with you, dearie."

Like a quilt slipping from the clothesline, Miss Becher folded slowly into a neat pile on the ground. I couldn't help myself. I started to laugh. Mr. Ware and Joshua joined in, and before I knew what had happened, we were all in a heap.

Sometimes when things get bad enough, laughing is about all you can do.

Twelve

"Mem," Papa called from the door. "Come inside and help your mama." Then he noticed Miss Becher on the ground and came rushing out. "What happened here?"

Mr. Ware scrambled to his feet. "I b'lieve the lady is overwrought."

Papa squatted down beside Miss Becher. "We seem to have more than our share of overwrought ladies." He tapped Miss Becher on the shoulder, but when she started to stir, he jumped up again. "Mem, you see to this lady. I'll go take care of your mother."

Joshua had crawled over close to Miss Becher and was busy looking up her nose.

As soon as Papa was back inside the cabin, Mr. Ware picked up his backpack. "I think I'd best be on my way before your teacher wakes up. Seems I have a powerful strong effect on her."

I reached up and caught his sleeve. "Oh, please, don't leave, Mr. Ware. I have so many more questions about hunting and trapping."

"You already know enough to keep yourself from going hungry. Don't expect me to tell you all my secrets, do you?" He patted my shoulder. "You'll do just fine."

"But will you stop by when you're coming back this way again?"

"You bet."

Mr. Ware waved and headed out toward the main road. When I couldn't see him anymore, I turned my attention to Miss Becher, elbowing Joshua out of the way and patting her lightly on the cheek. Her eyelids fluttered open. "Are you all right, Miss Becher? Did you hurt yourself?"

Miss Becher looked puzzled until her eyes focused on me and a look of panic crossed her face. She sat up and glanced around quickly. "Where is Mr. Turner? We really must be leaving."

"I'm afraid he left without you," I said.

Miss Becher's face crumpled, which disappointed me. I hadn't thought her to be such a ninny. She struggled to her feet and turned her back to me. I could tell she was wiping away tears. When she faced me again, her face was red but composed.

"I'm afraid you're stuck with us," I said, standing up myself.

She smiled, a little too brightly. "Well, then you're stuck with me, too, so I guess that makes us even."

"You can have my bed in the loft," I said, reaching for her bags. "I'll carry your things up the ladder for you."

She took the bags from me. "That's very kind of you, Remembrance, but I don't expect to be waited on. I'll help out with the work when I'm not at school. We can walk there together."

"I'm not coming back to school," I said. I waited for her to act surprised and remind me that I must get an education if I wanted to be a teacher.

But she only said, "Oh. Well, I'll see you when I come home after class, then."

Why didn't she say anything? Couldn't she see what a waste it would be for me to leave school? She must truly think me stupid.

I pushed the cabin door open slowly, not being sure in what condition I'd find Mama. Papa must have helped her dress, because the drawstring at her neckline was tied in a clumsy knot rather than a bow. Mama sat on the stool by the fire and smiled, but I could tell she wasn't with us.

"It's this way," I said, which was a stupid thing to say in a one-room cabin with only one ladder, but I just wanted to say something so that Miss Becher wouldn't notice there was something wrong with Mama. Then I remembered that Mama had made that perfectly clear to everyone outside.

Papa looked up. "This is my wife, Aurelia, Miss . . . I'm sorry."

"Miss Becher," I said.

"Emily Becher," she added, holding out her hand.

Papa took Mama's arm, and for one awful moment, I thought he was going to raise it himself for Miss Becher to shake, the way a child would introduce a doll. He must have realized what he was doing, because he stopped himself, letting Mama's arm drop limply to her lap. Mama just smiled, at nobody and nothing in particular.

Papa rushed over to us. "Here, let me take these." When he got the bags, he looked around helplessly.

"Miss Becher can have my bed, Papa."

"Yes, of course." Papa climbed far enough up the ladder to swing Miss Becher's bags into the loft, then backed down and stepped aside for us to pass.

I led the way. "This is my bed . . . your bed," I said, making another ridiculous observation, since the loft contained only my bed and a chest of drawers.

She opened the largest of her bags. "I have a quilt. I can sleep on the floor."

"No, I'll do that. Mama wouldn't have a guest sleep on the floor." I knew Mama wouldn't care if Miss Becher slept on the roof, but she would have cared once, and I wanted Miss Becher to know that. I pulled my quilt from the bed and helped Miss Becher spread it with hers. "I can empty a drawer for you," I offered.

"Don't bother, Mem. I can keep my things in my bags."

For a quick getaway, I thought.

Miss Becher's brow furrowed. "The older gentle-man . . . where does he stay?"

"Mr. Ware? He was just passing through."

"Oh." I saw the first look of genuine relief pass over her face.

I folded one of my quilts to make a mattress of sorts, then spread the other over it. "I'm going to start dinner now. I'll call you when it's ready."

"Can't I be of some help?"

"No, you rest for a bit. I can do it myself." I thought it was better to keep Miss Becher away from Mama as long as possible. It made as much sense as hoping people wouldn't notice that you had a bear in your parlor, but I couldn't help myself. Some part of me still believed that Mama would suddenly come back to her senses and I wouldn't have to worry about how to explain her to strangers.

I cooked the rabbit and fish the way Mr. Ware had shown me, stacking kindling outside in the same fire site he had used. Then I carried coals from the hearth to light my cooking fire. I suppose I could have figured out how to roast the rabbit on the hearth, but it had been a long time since I'd seen Mama cook meat. Besides, I hadn't paid much mind to how she'd done it, so it was easier to copy Mr. Ware's methods.

Before long, I had the rabbit meat roasting on a spit

and the fish frying in the long-legged skillet that Grandma called a spider. I cut slabs of cold mush and fried that up with the fish. All in all, it looked like a mighty tasty meal.

The smell of the food must have drawn Papa from the field to my cooking spot. "Where did you get all this, Mem?"

"I told you, Papa. Mr. Ware taught me how to snare and fish."

Papa leaned on his ax handle. "I was going to do that, but I've been too busy in the field. But if you want to amuse yourself by bringing in some food from the wild, I won't stop you. I'll be buying some feeder pigs in town, so we'll have real meat before long."

"This *is* real meat," I said. "And there's lots more where this came from. Pork isn't the only meat, you know."

Papa patted my head. "Never said it was. I just never developed much of a taste for game. Let me know when it's ready. I'll be splitting wood out back."

"Wait, Papa. Did you get the corn?" In all the excitement, I'd forgotten to ask.

"Not as much as I hoped for, Mem, but enough to replant the fields."

"You mean you don't have any that we can grind into meal?"

"We can live without cornmeal for a bit. If the weather holds, we'll bring in a good crop now. What with the fertile ground, it may take only half the time for corn to mature here as it did in New England." I didn't believe

him. I knew that in Connecticut it took the first half of
the summer for the corn to develop full ears and the rest
of the summer for it to dry on the cob. If that was Papa's
plan, we'd be long starved before he had anything to
feed us.

It made me angry that Papa acted like my efforts at
providing food were a child's game. If he had money for
feeder pigs, why hadn't he bought them before now? If
our sow, Sophie, hadn't been killed by a bear, she would
have had her piglets months ago. Every settler for miles
around must have been selling off extra pigs.

And if Papa knew how to set rabbit snares, why hadn't
he been doing that all along? It took only a few minutes
to set a snare. It wasn't as if you had to sit there in hiding, waiting for some poor unsuspecting rabbit to come
hopping along. Mr. Ware was right. Papa wasn't depend-
able. If I was the only sensible one left in the family, I'd
have to see that we never went hungry again.

I took the food inside, set the table, and quickly pinned
Mama's hair into a bun before I called Miss Becher. Then
I sent Joshua outside to fetch Papa.

Joshua ran back in just as Miss Becher was climbing
down the ladder. He pulled at my sleeve. "Mem, why was
that lady in your loft?"

"That's the teacher, Miss Becher. Didn't you hear Mr.
Turner say she'll be staying with us this month?"

Miss Becher came over to us, smiling.

"This is my little brother, Joshua," I said. "He hasn't been to school yet."

She leaned down and shook his hand. "I'm glad to meet you, Joshua."

He eyed her closely. "I never saw a teacher before."

"Oh? Do I look the way you expected a teacher to be?"

He considered the question for a minute, then shook his head. "I think you're supposed to have a pointed nose and frizzled hair."

Miss Becher laughed. "Did someone tell you that's what teachers look like, Joshua?"

"It certainly wasn't me," I said, pinching his arm.

Joshua pulled away from me. "Ow! Mem, that hurt!" He turned his attention back to Miss Becher. "I just always knew that about teachers, I think."

Miss Becher smiled. "Then I shall have to work on frizzing up my hair. I'm not sure I can do anything about my nose."

I shoved Joshua toward the table before he could start up with any new foolishness. "Let's all eat while the food is warm."

When we were seated, I looked to Mama to say the blessing, then decided I should take charge before she could get into any big sermon about the end of the world. I folded my hands and bowed my head. "We thank thee for our daily bread. Amen," I mumbled.

I spent the whole meal worrying about what Mama

might say to Miss Becher, what Joshua might say to Miss Becher, and even what Papa might say to Miss Becher. As it turned out, nobody said much of anything to anybody, because we were all so busy eating. All but Mama, who barely picked at her food. I didn't want to make a big fuss over getting Mama to eat in front of Miss Becher, but I'd try to coax her into eating more when we were alone during the day. The color had gone from her cheeks lately, and I heard her coughing during the night. She needed to stay healthy for Lily.

In spite of all my fretting, we managed to get through the meal without incident. And for someone with no taste for game, Papa made quick work of his share of the rabbit.

Thirteen

That night, Miss Becher helped me with the dishes while Mama sat at the table and stared into the fire.

Papa stood and stretched. "I got some seed potatoes today and want to get them planted, Mem. You see to things here."

We had just passed the longest day of the year. Now that it stayed light in the evening, we saw much less of Papa. There was always some chore or other that needed his attention.

When the dishes were dried and put away, I got Joshua to go to bed, then took out Mama's sewing basket and brought it to the table. I worked at mending a rip Mama had got in her blue dress at the camp meeting. The rip wasn't all that important, as Mama had no place to go, but I wanted to have something to do. Silence hung over the room like the heavy air before a rain.

Miss Becher tried to start a conversation. "I think I remember Mem telling me in school that your family moved here from Connecticut, Mrs. Nye."

Mama's eyes brightened a bit, and she nodded. "Connecticut," she said, in a voice that had gone husky from not being used.

"It's beautiful there," Miss Becher went on. "I once visited an aunt who lived right on the Connecticut River."

"Connecticut," Mama repeated, her eyes turning glassy with tears.

I reached over and patted Mama's hand as I gave Miss Becher a sharp look. Couldn't she see that she was upsetting Mama? "We still get homesick sometimes," I said, spreading the condition over the whole family instead of just Mama.

Miss Becher's fingers fussed nervously at the ruffle at her neck. "That's quite natural. I miss my home in Canandaigua, which is much closer than Connecticut."

At the third mention of home, Mama let out a soft moan.

Miss Becher jumped to her feet. "I'm feeling quite weary this evening. I think I'd like to retire early, Mem, although if you'd like to go first, I can wait."

"No, go ahead, Miss Becher. I have a few more chores to do."

That answered a question that had bothered me. I had wondered how Miss Becher and I would manage in the same sleeping quarters. It was one thing to be undressing in front of your own family, but would a teacher undress in front of one of her own pupils? And would I have to undress in front of her? It seemed improper to me. Now Miss Becher had made it clear that one of us would retire first, with the other going up after a suitable time. It surprised me that she hadn't assumed I would be the one to go first, me being a child. I decided that Mama must have made her so uncomfortable she simply couldn't bear to stay in the room.

After Miss Becher got all the way up the ladder, I woke Lily and took her to Mama. It was still light outside, but I decided we should all have an early night. I was so tired from all my chores these days, it seemed I never could get enough sleep. If she nursed now, Lily should sleep through almost to morning. If I waited until Lily woke on her own, it was too hard to rouse Mama in the middle of the night. Mama never gave Lily a thought anymore and didn't awaken to her cries.

As I lifted Lily, it occurred to me that she didn't seem to be getting any heavier, although I couldn't remember how quickly Joshua had grown when he was a babe or how big he was at one month. I feared that Lily wasn't getting enough milk. I wished I had someone I could ask about feeding her. I could trap and fish for the rest of us, but Lily needed Mama.

Lily had been sucking her thumb in her sleep, and her hair, moist with sweat, was curled in little half-moon ringlets around her face. I cradled her in my arms and wiped her forehead with the corner of my apron. She looked up at me and made gurgling noises. I kissed her on the nose and gurgled back to her. Her eyes were so bright when she looked at my face. I had heard that babies couldn't see anything this young, but I knew that wasn't true. Lily could already tell the difference between me and Mama.

"Mama. It's time to feed Lily."

Mama just stared, smiling a bit now, her homesickness forgotten. I longed to see the old Mama again, to have her scold and fuss at me. In the past, I'd seen Mama's eyes shoot sparks, but now if she looked at me at all, it was with those awful placid cow's eyes, which told me she had not a thought in her head.

"Mama, undo your dress and chemise. Lily needs to be nursed." She still did nothing, so I had to manage the drawstrings with one hand while I held Lily in the other arm. As Lily saw she was being handed to Mama, her face changed, taking on the same unseeing expression, as if she knew Mama cared little for her. I had to watch Mama now when she fed Lily, or she would set her back in her crib after only a few minutes and leave the poor babe screaming from hunger.

When she finished, I took Lily from her. Mama fumbled with the drawstring of her dress, starting to tie it up.

"It's late, Mama. Time to take off your dress and go to bed."

Mama undressed and climbed into bed like an obedient child. I changed Lily's clouts and put a fresh gown on

her. Then I took her over to the stool by the fire to cod-
dle her for a while. What with Artemus Ware and all the
excitement of Miss Becher coming, I had scarcely held
Lily today. I nuzzled her head and fluffed her fuzz of hair,
noticing that it was beginning to lighten. I guessed she
would be flaxen haired like Joshua before long.

I held Lily a long time, talking to her and letting her
grab my fingers. Then I started rocking on the stool,
watching her face as she drifted peacefully off to sleep.
"Poor Lily," I whispered. "You feel safe in my arms, but
what you don't know is that our family is completely
falling apart."

I only hoped Grandma would get here soon. I knew
when she saw Grandma, Mama could start to get better.
Maybe Grandma could convince Papa that we all should
go back home. The thought of being in Connecticut again
brought tears to my eyes. How I wished we'd never come
to this place.

I nuzzled Lily's head one last time and set her down in
her cradle. As I climbed the ladder, I was listening to hear
if she would wake up and cry. I did hear crying, but it
wasn't Lily. It was Miss Becher. She was curled up in the
bed with her back to me, her long braid stretched out
over the quilt.

I slipped off my dress and climbed into my bed of quilts
on the floor. Miss Becher must have heard me, because
the crying stopped. Then I realized she had been holding her breath for suddenly she let out a great sob.

"Are you all right, Miss Becher?"

She nodded but didn't say anything, and her shoulders shook with the effort of trying not to cry. Soon another sob escaped her.

"Would you like me to get you a cup of water?"

Miss Becher rolled over so I could see her face looking down at me from the bed. "I'm all right, Mem. I'm just homesick. I miss my mother."

"Just like my mama," I said. Then I realized Miss Becher wasn't just like Mama at all.

"Your poor mama is so far away from her family and hasn't seen them in over a year. I think I'd go mad if I were separated from . . ." She stopped, realizing what she had said.

"My grandmother is coming to stay with us," I said. "Mama will be fine once she's seen her again."

"That's wonderful, Mem. I'm sure she will." Miss Becher reached out to pull up her quilt, and I could see that she wore a real linen nightgown with crocheted lace on the sleeves instead of just going to bed in her chemise like Mama and me. Maybe she did that for modesty, because she had to live in other people's homes.

"Is it hard to be a teacher?" I asked. "Boarding out, I mean?"

"Some places are easier than others."

I wanted to ask if our house was one of the harder

places, but I was afraid I knew the answer. "Our last teacher left because she was homesick. She was from Canandaigua, just like you."

"I won't leave," Miss Becher said. "I made an agreement to teach for six months and I'll stick to it, no matter how much I miss my mother."

The thought came to me that Mama and Miss Becher weren't the only ones missing their mothers. Mama might be sleeping in the same cabin as me, but she wasn't the woman who had raised me. The fear that Mama might never be right in her head gripped me and I couldn't stop from crying.

Miss Becher saw my tears and reached down for my hand. "What's the matter, Mem?"

"I was just thinking that when you see your mother again, you'll be able to talk and carry on as if you've never been separated. I'm not sure I'll ever . . ."

My tears came in a rush now. Miss Becher squeezed my hand. "This must be very difficult for you, Mem. I had no idea you had so many responsibilities at home. But everything will be fine once your grandmother comes."

"I hope so," I said. "My mother isn't usually like this. It's just that things have been so hard for her here. And then with the awful weather—"

"Your mother will feel much better when it gets warmer. We all will."

"I guess so," I said.

Miss Becher smiled. "I'm sure of it. Now we should both get some sleep."

She squeezed my hand again, then let go and rolled over, leaving me to lie awake and worry about Mama. I could hear Mama coughing in her bed. Now she'd probably taken cold from not dressing for the weather. That gave me one more thing to worry about. I was still awake when I heard Papa come in from the field.

The next morning I rose before dawn, milked Chloe, gathered eggs, made the breakfast, and packed a tin of fried mush and a hard-cooked egg for Miss Becher's lunch. "It's all I have for now," I said, "but I'll try to catch more fish and rabbits so there will be meat left over from dinner for you to take tomorrow."

Miss Becher took the lunch pail from me. "This will be fine, Mem. Thank you."

I watched her walk toward the school. She wore a deep green dress today, and I thought how pretty that color would look on Mama with her chestnut hair. If I ever had some money, I'd buy some green cloth for Mama to make herself a dress.

After I cleaned up the breakfast, I got Mama to nurse Lily, then set Joshua off to find the eggs I'd missed. "Mind you look carefully for the eggs, Joshua. The hens are trying to go broody."

"What's broody?" he asked.

"The hens want to hatch out their eggs to raise chicks. There are two hens setting on nests behind the woodpile. Leave those be, but bring in any eggs you find in other places."

I went to check my line of rabbit snares and found them empty. I knew we needed the meat, but deep down I was relieved not to have to kill and dress out another rabbit. I did manage to catch two trout, and even though I didn't like to clean them, the prospect of a good meal made it worth the effort.

I hauled water up from the creek and set the kettle over a fire outside to heat for laundry. Mama always had certain days for doing chores, but I was just trying to keep us fed and clothed, never mind what day it was.

Papa had built a bench in the yard to hold the washtub. I was scrubbing Papa's shirt on the washboard when Mama came out. She had braided her own hair but let it hang loose instead of coiling it up in a bun. "Mind you get the soap rinsed out of those clothes, or you'll set us all to itching."

It was so good to hear her voice again. I had almost forgotten what it sounded like. "I'll rinse them well, Mama. I'll do it in the creek."

She came over and stood behind me. "You'll have to scrub harder than that to get the dirt out." She watched for a minute, then took the shirt from my hands and began scrubbing it herself. "Things get so dirty here. It barely pays to wash them. They'll be filthy again before you know it."

"I think this one is almost clean, Mama."

She scrubbed faster. "I try so hard . . ." She was crying now, and I saw that she had rubbed her knuckles so vigorously on the washboard, they were beginning to bleed. "I never wanted to come here. . . ." She dropped the shirt in the tub and wiped her eyes, getting soap into them. She staggered back a few steps from the tub, sobbing, then dropped to her knees.

I knelt next to her and pulled her over to my lap. "It's all right, Mama."

"No, it isn't all right!" Mama cried, dissolving into sobs.

"Shhh," I whispered, smoothing back her hair. "Grandma's coming soon, remember?"

If she did remember, she gave no sign of it. She wailed with a sound coming from so deep inside, I feared that anything left of the Mama I knew would come spilling out and disappear forever. I wished desperately for something that would help her last until Grandma arrived. Then I remembered.

I reached under the neck of my dress and took off the locket. It gleamed in the sunlight. "Grandma gave this to me just before we left home. Look what's inside." I opened the locket and showed her the three auburn curls. "One of the locks is Grandma's, one is her grandmother's, and one is mine."

Mama cradled the locket in her hand and gently touched the curls of hair. "Mama?" she whispered.

"This is what she did when she gave it to me," I said. I still had the scissors from Mama's sewing kit in my apron pocket. I snipped a curl from the end of her braid and nestled it in with the others. "Grandma told me this was to remind me of my connections to family." I closed the locket and fastened the clasp around Mama's neck. "Don't worry. Grandma's coming," I said, and I kissed her on the cheek.

Fourteen

Over the next few weeks, my life settled into a pattern of working from the time I got up in the morning until I fell into bed, exhausted, at night. I had never realized how hard Mama worked all day. Now I was doing all of her chores with the added responsibility of fishing and hunting. I had managed to catch a fish or two almost every day, but my snares had remained empty. I wished I could talk to Mr. Ware again to find out what I was doing wrong. I had a feeling that the rabbits had started a new trail, but I couldn't find any signs of it. As much as I didn't relish the thought of killing and skinning a rabbit, I was getting powerful sick of fish.

Mama no longer made any attempt to help with household chores or tend to Lily. She seemed tired even though she did nothing all day, and her cough still lingered. On pleasant days, I'd lead her outside to sit on the

bench near her flower garden, but she showed no interest in it.

I taught Joshua how to help with some of the chores,
but Chloe wouldn't let him milk her. I couldn't trust him
with the cooking, as he would let his mind wander, burning the mush to the bottom of the pot or charring the
fish on the spider. Food was too scarce now to risk losing
it. It amazed me to think that I had become the expert
cook in the family.

Joshua had learned to be very good at caring for Lily,
though. I knew I could leave her with him and he would
carry her around, talking to her constantly until I got
back. It brought me a pang to see Lily's face light up more
to the sight of Joshua than to me now, but I was grateful
for his help.

Papa had planted the corn but decided to leave some
out for us to grind for meal. I handled it as if it were precious as gold, carefully picking every last grain out of the
mortar when I finished. After some fine weather, we had
frost again the second week of July, but the corn hadn't
burst forth from the ground yet, so it wasn't killed this
time. The weather soon warmed, and it seemed as if
summer had finally arrived. Lily was six weeks old and
seemed to be thriving. I was foolish enough to think that
our troubles might almost be over.

Then one morning I realized that Miss Becher had
gone off to school and left her lunch box. I thought of
sending Joshua with it, but I knew it would take him half

the day to walk the mile out to the post road and almost two more miles into town, stopping to examine everything he found interesting along the way. I had caught up with my chores for the moment and decided I'd enjoy the outing to Williamson myself. Besides, I was eager to check the post office for Grandma's letter. It had been over a month since I'd written to her. Surely her answer would arrive any day now.

"Joshua," I said. "I have to take Miss Becher's lunch to her. I won't be long."

"May I go, too, Mem?"

"No. You must stay home and take care of Mama and Lily."

"Oh, please, Mem? Pleeeease? Mama and Lily don't need me."

I looked over at Lily, who was napping in her cradle. Mama was sleeping soundly in her bed, except for an occasional cough. I didn't like the sound of her breathing, as it had a slight rattle to it now. Still, the cough didn't seem to disturb her sleep. Both Mama and Lily often dozed for the better part of the morning after the nursing.

I thought about having to go into the schoolhouse myself and walk past the mocking eyes of Hannah's friend and the Crowell boys. Maybe it would be a good idea to have Joshua along to make the delivery. If we kept a good pace, we could go to Williamson and be back in plenty of time for me to make the noonday meal. Mama and Lily would probably sleep the whole time.

I went outside and looked back toward the field, but Papa was nowhere in sight. Still, he usually checked back at the cabin at least once during the morning, so if anything was amiss, he'd handle it. The weather was cold and sour. I hoped we weren't in for another frost.

I put another log on the fire and wrapped Lily in a woolen cloth to keep her warm in case the fire went out. Then I picked up the lunch tin. "All right, Joshua. You may come with me, but we mustn't dawdle."

"I can walk as fast as you now, Mem." He started off ahead to prove his point. I took one last look at Mama and Lily, then closed the door quietly behind me.

Joshua kept up his show of strength all the way out to the post road, but he began fading as he walked toward Williamson, so it wasn't long before I caught up to him.

"That was fast walking, wasn't it, Mem?"

"Yes, Joshua. But you need to keep going."

I was beginning to wish that I'd taken my shawl. The weather was turning colder, and clouds hung dark overhead. I hoped it wouldn't get cold enough to hurt our corn. The crop was almost a hand high already.

I could just see the buildings of Williamson up ahead when a wagon pulled away from the tavern and headed toward us. It didn't take long for me to make out the grim countenance of the driver. I grabbed Joshua's arm and pulled him behind a tree.

"What's the matter, Mem?"

"Mrs. Foster is coming. I don't want her to see us."

"Is that the lady who took us to the camp meeting?" he whispered.

I put my hand on his shoulder. "Yes. Be still." I felt a little shiver go through him as the wagon went by, its wheels spitting loose stones and twigs at us.

"Is she going to see Mama?"

"I doubt that, Joshua. Papa spoke harshly to her at the camp meeting. She'll think twice before she bothers us again." I thought back to the first time Mrs. Foster had visited. Mama had been so happy to serve tea to a guest, even though it was only the Oswego tea used by the settlers. How I wished I had the money to buy some real tea for Mama now. I could just picture how pleased she'd be, inhaling the fragrant steam before she took a sip. I wondered how much it would cost to buy just enough tea for one cup.

"Mem! Wait for me!" Joshua's cries made me realize I had started off at a fast pace, but I couldn't slow down. I was going to ask Major Ballard to let me work for the price of a cup of tea.

Joshua was out of breath from running as we reached the tavern steps. I handed him the lunch tin. "That log cabin next door is the schoolhouse. Take this to Miss Becher."

"Shall I tell her it's her lunch?"

"She'll know, Joshua. Don't dally around in there. Give her the lunch and tell her you have to come right back. I'll meet you on these steps." Just seeing the schoolhouse reminded me of the humiliation I'd suffered there, and I was glad I didn't have to be seen by the other students.

"Major Ballard?" I called as I entered the tavern.

He appeared from behind the bar, wiping his hands on a towel. "Ah, Remembrance Nye, isn't it?"

"Yes, sir," I said.

"And what can I do for you today?"

"My mother has been feeling poorly and I want to cheer her up, sir. I was wondering if you could sell me enough real tea to make just one cup? And could I work for the money to earn it?"

He smiled and pulled a tin from the shelf. "I've always felt a cup of good tea can set the world in order when things have gone awry—especially on a day like this. Tea is best when shared, though. Wouldn't you like enough so you could join your mother?" He handed me the broom that had been leaning in the corner. "I think a good floor sweeping should earn enough tea for two cups."

I took the broom eagerly. "Yes, sir. There'll not be a speck of dirt left on your floor when I've finished." I set to work right away. It was a pleasure to sweep a wood floor, compared to the dirt one at home. I never could see the sense in sweeping a dirt floor. I could smooth it out with the broom, but my own footsteps messed it up again as I worked.

I moved the tavern chairs and tables to sweep under them, all but the one where two men argued about the weather. I tried to sweep around them without disturbing their conversation.

"It's the sunspots causing the cold, Daniel," the tall one said. "There was one the other day so big you could see it with the naked eye. In the shape of a bee it was, clear as anything."

"Amasa, that's nonsense and you know it. How in tarnation could a spot on the sun make the weather cold? Didn't stop the sun from rising in the sky, did it?"

"Oh, you know better than what's in the newspapers, do you? Just last week the *Ontario Repository* had a report from Philadelphia that every time the weather gets cold like this, soon after there are spots on the sun."

Daniel tapped his pipe on the chair leg, knocking ashes where I had just swept. "Well, listen to yourself, man. The weather comes before the spots, not after it. I'm telling you, the trouble is right here on earth, not on the sun."

Amasa leaned forward on the table, making it easier for me to sweep behind his chair. Though I knew it was wrong to eavesdrop, I wanted to hear Daniel's answer, too. "How so?" he asked.

Daniel took the time to light his pipe, so I pretended to sweep at a stubborn spot on the floor to stay nearby. "It was that blasted Ben Franklin," he said finally. "The earth is warmed by the fluid electricity running through the ground, right?"

Amasa nodded. "I've heard tell of that."

"Well, Benjamin Franklin started this whole thing when he invented the lightning rod. Those confounded things have sprouted up on barns all over the country. They're interrupting the natural flow of electricity. That's why it's been so blasted cold. Get people to throw away them confounded lightning rods and you stop the bad weather."

I wished I had known those arguments about the weather back when Mrs. Foster was trying to convince Mama that the world was coming to an end. I'd be sure to tell Mama what I'd heard. Maybe it would ease her mind a bit. I finished up the last of the sweeping and put the broom back.

Major Ballard took two good-sized pinches of tea from the tin, dropped them on a paper, and folded it into a neat packet. "You're a fast worker, Remembrance. Here's your pay. I hope this makes your mother feel better, although the letter you got today might help, too. If I'd known you were coming, I'd have saved it for you."

"There was a letter for me? What happened to it?"

"Well, it was addressed to your mother. As I said, I would have saved it for you if I'd known . . ."

"You sent it back?"

Major Ballard laughed. "No, of course not. I merely sent it on to your mother with a friend. I was sure she'd be anxious to get it."

"Which friend?" I asked, dreading the answer.

"Why, it was Mrs. Foster. She saw the letter in your box and said your mother had been waiting for it."

"My mother told her no such thing," I said. "Mrs. Foster is not a friend."

Major Ballard shook his head. "People often pick up mail for their neighbors, but I should have known that old busybody was just being meddlesome. She has to know everybody's business. And she'd run your life if you let her."

"I know," I said. "But I don't understand what she wants with my mother."

"It's because she has no family of her own anymore. She's a widow with three married daughters who packed up and moved farther west. I always suspected they wanted to get away from their mother's meddling. Most people around here are wise to her and keep their distance, but she's always looking for some unsuspecting new settler to latch onto. I can't help but feel sorry for her. I'm sure she means well."

In spite of Major Ballard's assurances, I still felt the need to get home as quickly as possible. The letter had given Mrs. Foster an excuse to visit Mama in spite of Papa telling her to stay away. Having a guest, no matter who it was, might confuse and frighten Mama.

"Thank you for the tea," I said. I tucked the small packet into my pocket and ran out to the tavern steps. I looked for Joshua, but he wasn't there yet even though I'd spent all that extra time sweeping the floor.

I ran over to the schoolhouse and looked in the window. There was Joshua, playing the clown in the front of the room with Miss Becher. She was being indulgent with him, probably because of boarding with us. Now that he was the center of attention, it would be harder than ever to get him out of there.

I burst through the back door. "Joshua. Come here this minute."

He looked up, his face flushed. "But I like school, Mem. I want to stay."

"You're too young," I said.

Miss Becher put her hand on his shoulder. "Actually he could start his schooling now, Mem. At least he can stay with me today. I'll bring him home with me."

I didn't have time to argue. Besides, without Joshua dragging me down, I could get home faster. "All right," I said. "Just behave, Joshua."

I started running toward home. If I paced myself, I should be able to run most of the way. I was glad Major Ballard had told me about Mrs. Foster. Now that I knew she was nothing more than a lonely old woman, I didn't fear her. After all, if she really believed the world was ending, she thought she was doing us a favor by taking us to the camp meeting. A small part of me was still wary of her, though. Major Ballard might see Mrs. Foster as a harmless old woman, but she had managed to carry my whole family off with her the last time we'd met. This time I'd be polite, but prepared for the worst.

I was less than halfway down the road when I had such a sharp stitch in my side, I had to stop running. I tried to walk as fast as I could, pressing my hand into my ribs to stop the pain.

That's when I started thinking about the letter. It had to be from Grandma. Surely the good news would make Mama happy. How could the world be coming to an end if Grandma was on her way to us?

I started running again. "Hold on, Mama," I whispered. "Don't listen to Mrs. Foster's tales of doom."

Just then I heard the sound of horse's hooves. A wagon was coming toward me. As it got nearer, I could see that it was Mrs. Foster. I stepped off the side of the road, but she spotted me and stopped.

"I thought it was you," Mrs. Foster shrieked. "Why are you gadding about? You should be home watching over your crazy mother."

"My mother is not crazy."

Mrs. Foster jutted out her chin. "Oh, no? Well, her rudeness tells me otherwise. I went out of my way to deliver a letter to her, but did she even thank me? Not one word." She cracked her whip and the horse charged past me, almost knocking me off my feet.

I ran for home now, ignoring the searing pain in my side. I found the cabin door open. Mama and Lily weren't there. She must have gone to the field to tell Papa about Grandma's letter. I couldn't wait to read it myself. Hearing from Grandma would be the next best thing to seeing her. And if she had started out right after sending the letter, she might be here any day.

Papa was kneeling in the field, looking at the corn, but Mama and Lily were nowhere in sight.

"Papa!" I called with what little breath I had left.

He looked up as I ran to him. "The best crop I've ever grown and the temperature is dropping. Do you feel it?"

"Yes, Papa, but . . ."

"I've never seen corn grow so fast. And look at the color of the leaves—a healthy dark green. Our corn never looked like this at home. But if we get another frost tonight, we'll lose it all."

"Papa, where is Mama? Did she show you the letter?"

"I haven't seen your mother." For the first time, he turned his full attention to me. "What do you mean, Mem? You didn't leave your mother alone, did you?"

"Well, I had to take Miss Becher's lunch to her. I was only gone for a short time, and Mama and Lily were sleeping when we left."

Papa stood up. "*We* left? You went all the way into Williamson and took Joshua with you?"

I nodded, realizing for the first time how foolish I had been.

"Tarnation, child! What were you thinking? You know your mother can't be left alone. There's no telling where she's gone. Where is the babe? Did you leave her alone in the cabin just now?"

"No, Papa, she's gone. Mama must have taken Lily with her."

It wasn't until I said the words out loud that I knew how awful their meaning could be.

"Where was your head, Mem?" Papa shouted. "You're supposed to watch your mother at all times! You know that!"

"I'm sorry, Papa. I just . . ."

"Where's Joshua? Have you gone and lost him, too?"

"No, he's fine. Miss Becher has him at the schoolhouse."

Papa headed for the cabin. "You were gone for how long? An hour?"

It was longer than that, but I didn't need to tell Papa. "She can't have gotten very far. There hasn't been enough time. Mrs. Foster just delivered a letter to her."

Papa stopped in his tracks. "The woman from the camp meeting? Do you think your mother went off with her?"

"No, I'm sure she didn't. I just saw Mrs. Foster on the road, and Mama wasn't in the wagon. I don't know why Mama would leave."

"Who knows what your mother is thinking? We'll begin back at the cabin. Maybe she came to her senses enough to leave a note."

He called Mama's name all the way back to the cabin

and walked with such long strides, I had to run every few steps to keep up. As we burst through the door, I half expected to see Mama there, startled by our noisy entrance. But she wasn't there and neither was Lily. And there was no note.

Papa sat at the table, put his head in his hands, and rubbed his forehead. "All right, I have to think this out for a minute. We can't just be running off in all directions."

"We need help," I said. "We should have other people looking for her, too."

Papa frowned. "I don't want to be bringing strangers into our family affairs."

"Papa, there are miles of wilderness out there. If Mama didn't hear us call just now, she could be anywhere. We don't have any way to know which direction she went."

Papa took a deep breath and let it out. "All right. Go to the postmaster in Williamson and tell him to spread the news. I'll do the same thing in Pultneyville. If she stays on the roads, it should be easy to spot her. If she's gone off into the woods . . ." He let his voice trail off, but I understood his meaning and was glad he didn't speak the words.

"But I would have seen her on the road to Williamson, Papa. Shouldn't I look for her in the woods instead?"

Papa stood up so suddenly, he knocked the bench over. "And then we'd have three members of the family lost? Use your head, Mem. You can reach more people in that tavern than you could any other place for miles. What we need are people who have lived here longer than us. People who know the lay of the land."

"All right, Papa." As I picked up my shawl, I noticed that Mama had left hers. And worse yet, Lily's blanket lay in her cradle. I hoped Lily was still wrapped in the wool cloth I had put on her, but I shivered to think that Mama wore nothing to protect herself from the cold.

Fifteen

Papa had already started toward Pultneyville by the time I reached the main road. I could hear him calling Mama's name as he walked. I tried to do the same, but before long, I was breathless from running. I stopped at the two farms along the way and told the men working in the fields about Mama and Lily. Nobody had seen them. The man at the second farm unhitched his horse from the plow right then and rode me the rest of the way into Williamson.

"Major Ballard!" I called as I burst into the tavern.

He was behind the bar when I came in but moved over to the store and post office section to talk to me. "What is it, child?"

"It's my mother. She's gone off somewhere with my baby sister. We need help to find her."

Major Ballard smiled. He reached into the candy jar

and handed me a peppermint drop. "You were here not much more than an hour ago. Your mama probably felt better and went out to visit a neighbor. No need to get all worked up over nothing. I'm sure she'll be home directly."

"No, you don't understand," I said. Amasa and Daniel were still at their table and had been joined by a third man. They had stopped talking to eavesdrop on our conversation, but our family secrets didn't matter anymore. People had to know about Mama, or they wouldn't see the need to search. "Mama gets confused. She could be right near our cabin and not know where she was." I took a deep breath and blurted out the whole truth. "Mama is going mad. And she doesn't seem to know how to care for the baby. She might just put Lily down somewhere and forget her." There, I said it. Hearing my own words made me shiver inside.

Major Ballard reached out and touched my shoulder. "I had no idea. We'll get people out there searching right away."

Daniel stood up and gulped the last of his whiskey. "We'll go now. Where's the cabin?"

Major Ballard gave them directions and the three set out. A cold rain was starting as I stepped outside.

I tried to think of where Mama could have gone. Would she head out to meet Grandma? If so, she would have to come to Williamson to meet the stagecoach. I decided to go through the town, knocking on doors, telling people about my mother. With each person I told, my spirits rose a bit. After all, the more people we had searching, the sooner we'd find her. I vowed to myself that I'd never leave Mama's side again. This was all my fault.

By the time I was back at the tavern, a number of people had gathered and they were planning which areas each of them would search. A woman from a house where I had just stopped ran over to me. She carried a pair of boots and some wool stockings. "You take these, dear. Your feet must be about to freeze. I think they'll fit you."

"Thank you," I said. "I'll bring them back tomorrow, if that's all right."

The woman shook her head. "No need to return them. They were my daughter's. She has no more use for them."

I went into the tavern to get out of the rain and put on the boots and stockings. The boots were better than any I had ever had and fit as well as if they had been made for me. As I laced them up, I thought about Hannah's promise to give me her outgrown shoes. She and her family would be helping us to find Mama now if they hadn't moved away.

A crowd had gathered in the tavern, and all the talk was about Mama. I heard Major Ballard say, "You must have been the last one to see her. Did she say what was in the letter? Did she say where she was going?"

I pushed my way through the crowd. There was Mrs. Foster. The old busybody must have come in to see what all the ruckus was about.

I lunged at her. "What did you do to my mama?" I screamed. I grabbed the black ribbon on her bonnet, yanking it down over her crow's beak before Major Ballard caught my arms and held me back. "Easy, child. Let the adults handle this." Mama would have been mortified by my terrible behavior, but I didn't care. If the old crow had said something to confuse or frighten Mama, I wanted to know about it.

"There, you see?" Mrs. Foster sputtered as she settled her bonnet back in place. "Madness runs in the family. The mother is completely insane. I went out of my way to deliver a letter to her and she never said a word. Not one word."

"Did she seem upset when she read the letter?" Major Ballard persisted. "Even if she didn't speak, could you tell by her face?"

"She just stared." Mrs. Foster looked over at me. "I doubt she's even able to read. The child is illiterate, too, I hear."

"You horrible old crow," I shouted. I tried to struggle loose from Major Ballard to get at her, but he pulled me out of the crowd and over to the door.

"I know you're angry, Remembrance, but we're losing precious time. Go back home now so you can show the searchers where your mother might have gone. I'll see if I can get any more information out of the old crow." He smiled and winked at me.

As I went back out into the rain and wind, I could smell smoke coming from the chimney of the schoolhouse next door. I should tell Miss Becher what happened and take Joshua back home. The wind was blowing the rain sideways now, but even though my shawl and dress were soaked clean through, I was too numb to feel the cold.

I went inside the schoolhouse without knocking and stood in the back of the room. Joshua spotted me right away. "I'm not going home yet, Mem. I like school."

Miss Becher looked up and came to me. "What is it, Mem?"

"Mama's gone," I said. "She's taken Lily with her. They're organizing a search over at the tavern." My voice cracked at the last of this, and I started to cry.

Miss Becher pulled me close and rested my head on her shoulder. "They'll find her, Mem. Come by the fire and warm up." As she led me to the front of the room by the fireplace, I noticed that my sopping clothes had left a wet stain on one side of her dress.

The whole room was buzzing with talk, but she silenced everyone by raising her hand. "Boys and girls, I'm dismissing school for the day."

The Crowell brothers bolted for the door, but she stopped them. "Wait! Mem has just told me that her mother and baby sister are lost. The men of the town are out searching for them. I want you all to go home and tell your parents we need help in the search. And those of you who live away from the center of town, stop and tell your neighbors along the way. Her name is Aurelia. They should call it out so as not to frighten her."

As the room emptied, Joshua ran to me. "Mem! Where have they gone? Is Lily all right?"

Miss Becher caught him up in her arms. "Many people are out searching, Joshua. They'll find Lily and your mother."

"But there's nothing but wilderness out there," I said. "How can they find her if she's off the road?"

"People do get lost in these woods, Mem. Your mother isn't the first. The settlers around here know where to look."

Miss Becher's attempt to comfort me brought tears to my eyes again. Joshua ran over and clung to my skirts. "Don't cry, Mem. Mama and Lily will be all right. Miss Becher said so." It made me angry that Joshua could believe everything he was told so easily while I was tortured with worry.

Miss Becher gathered her things and put out the fire. "Come now," she said. "Let's get home."

The freezing rain hit us full in the face as we went out into the street. Miss Becher pulled her shawl over Joshua and offered to do the same for me, but I shook my head. "I can't get any wetter than I am now," I said.

Before we even reached the crossroads, a carriage pulled over. A woman I didn't know leaned out to call to us. "Are those the lost woman's children?"

Miss Becher nodded.

"Get in, then," said the woman. "I'm taking a pot of stew to their house."

The woman reached down to help us into the carriage, first Miss Becher, then Joshua, then me. "I'm Ethel Myers," she said as she gripped my hand. "I'm sorry about your mother. If I'd known what was going on with her, I could have helped."

"Nothing was going on," I said.

She put her hand on my shoulder. "It's all right, child. There's no shame to it. It's a wonder we don't all go mad in this place."

I felt my face turn hot. How Mama would hate to have people talking about her like this.

When we got home, there were as many people as we had on the day of our cabin raising. Inside, strange women poked at the fire and stirred kettles with soup and stew. But without Mama and Lily, the room seemed cold and empty. I had to go look for them.

As I started to leave, one of the women caught my hand. "Don't go out in this weather, child. You'll catch your death."

"I need to find my mother," I said.

The woman pulled me back into the cabin and over to the fire. She unwound the sodden shawl from my shoulders. "Let the men do the searching. You don't want your mother to come back and find you gone, do you?"

She meant well, but she had the same smile and tone of voice that mothers use when they are lying to children or telling them fairy stories. I could tell by the way she avoided my eyes that she didn't think Mama would ever come back.

I let someone take off my dress and wrap me in a dry quilt. Then a pair of hands handed me a bowl of steaming stew with carrots, potatoes, and venison. I wept at the thought that I was warm while Mama and Lily were out somewhere in the icy rain.

A large woman with big hands pulled me onto her lap and started spooning the stew into my mouth. It was Ethel Myers, the woman who had given us a ride home. At first I shook my head and wouldn't take any. Didn't she understand that I didn't deserve this? That Mama and Lily being lost was my fault?

I looked across the room and saw that Joshua was receiving the same treatment, but he was gobbling his food gratefully and even smiling as he did it. Joshua hadn't a brain in his head.

I finally managed to choke down some of the stew, as the woman wasn't going to give up until I did. Then she held my head down to her shoulder and started singing a song—a lullaby—in some language I didn't understand. I sobbed quietly into the strange shoulder and felt as if I had become a small babe again, with no one depending on me for anything. The voices around me faded into a hum and the hum became part of the woman's song. I could feel myself being carried away into sleep.

That's when I heard Lily crying in my dream. It was faint at first, then it became louder. I was standing out in the middle of a blizzard, but I wasn't cold. "Lily?" I called out. "Is that you?" I whirled around to find the source of the crying, but it seemed to be coming from all directions at once. Then I stepped forward into the blinding snow. My foot slipped and suddenly I was sliding off a rocky ledge. I could feel branches whipping against my face as I fell. I reached out to get a handhold, but nothing would stop me as I plunged into the icy darkness.

Sixteen

When I woke up, I was in my bed. Miss Becher was sleeping soundly in quilts on the floor. I hadn't remembered seeing her from the time we arrived at the cabin. Everything had melted into a blur, and it was hard to tell which parts were real and which parts were a dream. I prayed that the part about Mama and Lily being lost was only a bad dream, but when I climbed down the ladder, I knew the truth.

In the dim light from the fire, I could see people sleeping all over the floor. Three women were in Mama and Papa's bed, and Lily's cradle was empty. Papa slept on the floor next to Joshua's cot. The other faces were strange to me. These people must have searched until darkness or later, then stayed so as to begin searching in the morning. That meant Lily and Mama were alone in the cold and darkness and nobody was trying to find them.

I found my dress and the new boots and stockings by the fire, now dry and warm. I dressed silently, wrapped myself in my shawl, and took Mama's shawl and Lily's blanket. I slipped a piece of Indian bread from the table into my pocket, then went back to get a second piece. Mama would be hungry when I found her.

I opened the door as quietly as possible, but I saw a man waken with the squeak of the hinge. I couldn't bear to be held back from searching again. I closed the door carefully behind me and started running toward the cornfield.

The crunching sound made by my footsteps could mean only one thing. The first light of dawn showed the ground coated with silvery frost again. Even from a distance, I could see that the corn lay dead and blackened for the third time in the field. That meant that unless Mama and Lily had found shelter, they had been out all night in a killing frost.

Mr. Ware had said that in order to snare a rabbit, you had to think like a rabbit. But how could I think like Mama? I didn't know why she left the cabin. At first I thought it was because she was happy about Grandma coming, but if that was true, she would have gone to share the news with Papa.

Now I feared that the letter said something else—that Grandma was sick and couldn't make the journey. My throat tightened with fear at that thought. Mama would have been confused and frightened. Her first thought would be to go home to Grandma, but she wouldn't think about the sensible way to go—on the roads. Mama had always been good at calculating directions without having to look at a compass. She had once said to me that Connecticut lay to the southeast of us, and she had pointed the way. What if she had simply faced the southeast yesterday and set out for home?

The rising sun told me where east was, so I set a course to the south of that and started walking. Somewhere from deep inside, I could still hear Lily's cries from the dream. I headed farther into the woods, in a direction I'd never gone before. It wasn't sensible for Mama to have come this way, so the searchers probably hadn't looked in this area. I called out Mama's name every few steps.

Most of the leaves on the trees had blackened and shriveled from the frost, which let more light reach the ground. I kept going, watching for clues to show that someone had come through here, but I could find nothing. The new frost had concealed everything with its glistening surface.

Even in dry clothes and wrapped in a shawl, the cold settled in right to my bones. Mama wore only her chemise and a thin dress. She would be wet from last night's icy rain. Would she remember to keep the woolen cloth wrapped tight around Lily? Even wet, the wool could keep Lily warm.

A picture flashed through my mind of Mama setting

Lily down on the ground, then wandering off and leaving her behind. "Oh, Mama," I said out loud. "Please, take care of Lily. Don't forget her." I started walking faster.

The sound of Lily's cries still echoed through my head, but it seemed different now. The cry was more muffled, but I suddenly realized there was a real baby crying somewhere nearby, and there was also the sound of rushing water.

"Lily!" I screamed. "Mama! Where are you?"

The cry seemed to be coming from beyond a rise. I ran to it and found a stream on the other side, but no sign of Mama or Lily. And now that I was close to the rapidly coursing water, I couldn't hear the baby crying anymore.

Ice had formed by the edges where the water was shallow and still. As I looked along the bank, my eyes fell on a place where the ice was broken. Had Mama and Lily fallen through? I looked from the punched-out section to the opposite bank, where there was another patch of broken ice. Someone had crossed the stream here. Was it Mama, or had it only been a deer, coming in for a drink? Had I only imagined the baby's cry?

That's when I saw her. Mama was sitting hunched over, leaning against the trunk of a tree a short distance away. "Mama!" I called. "Mama, are you all right?"

She didn't raise her head. She probably couldn't hear me over the sound of the water and Lily's cries. Mama had her arms wrapped around Lily and was leaning close to her, trying to soothe her.

"I'm coming, Mama!" I waded into the stream, my heart thudding against my chest. For the first two steps, it was only ankle deep, but with the next step I was almost up to my knees in the icy water. The shock of it took my breath away and knocked me off-balance. Then the current tugged at my skirts, but I managed to grab a branch from the opposite bank to pull myself up out of the water. My legs had gone numb from the cold, but none of that mattered now that I had found Mama.

I ran to her, my sodden skirts slapping against my legs, and dropped to my knees by her side. Lily was screaming, and all I could see of her was her little fist waving above the blanket. Mama had kept her wrapped up and safe and had sheltered her from the cold with her own body. But Mama wore only her threadbare linen dress and it was soaked almost up to her waist, the folds of her skirt stiff with frost.

I gently shook her shoulder. "Mama? Mama, can you hear me?" When she didn't respond, I spoke louder and shook a little harder. "Mama, wake up! It's Mem. Everything will be all right now." Nothing I did seemed to rouse her. She was too weak to open her eyes.

"Let me take Lily for you and I'll go for help." I brushed Mama's hair away from her face. Her skin was pale, and she felt half frozen. I reached over and slipped Lily from Mama's arms. "I'm going for help, Mama. It won't take long. I'll run all the way."

I hated to leave her all alone, but I couldn't carry

her across the creek and back to the cabin by myself. I wrapped Mama's shawl around her shoulders and added my own. "Here, Mama. This will keep you warm until I come back."

Crossing through the creek, I planted each foot cautiously, testing it before I shifted my weight. Lily was cradled in one arm and I kept hold of a branch with the other for as long as I could. Then I grabbed a branch from the opposite bank to steady me the rest of the way. After scrambling up the other side, I stopped to get my bearings, noting landmarks so I could tell others where to find Mama.

I started out running, but my feet were so numb from the cold water, they made my steps unsure. I was afraid I'd trip and sprawl headlong on top of Lily, so I settled for a fast walk, all the while planning how I would care for Mama once she was safe at home. "I'll get Mama's quilts and mine from the loft and warm them all by the fire," I told Lily, as if she could understand. "I'll make them into a fine bed near the hearth."

I held Lily close, nuzzling her cheek as I walked. She had quieted down, soothed by the sound of my voice, so I kept talking to her as we hurried through the woods. "Then as soon as Mama wakes up, I'll give her a special surprise, Lily—a cup of real tea like she used to have in Connecticut. I can't wait to see her face when she tastes it."

I was warm in front, where I held Lily tight to my

chest, but the cold wind bit through the thin dress over my back and shoulders. I had been walking long enough for the hem of my skirt to stiffen with ice when I heard two men talking nearby. My cries for help brought them running. "You've found the babe!" the older one said. "Is she all right?"

"Yes," I said. "But my mother needs help. She's too weak to walk. Go straight back from here to the creek. There's a maple split in half by lightning where she waded through the water, and she's just beyond that."

"Don't worry, child," the older man said. "We can follow your wet footprints in the frost. We'll find her and carry her home." The two men started off, running.

I picked up my pace as I neared the cabin. Mama was going to be all right, and I vowed to take better care of her in the future. I'd surely never leave her alone again.

Several women gathered around me as I went inside. I shook them away and wouldn't let them take Lily from me. I needed to hold on to her for a minute just to remind myself that she was safe. Mrs. Myers looked concerned. "Did the men find your mother, Mem?"

"No, I found her. I told them where she is. They'll be bringing her back directly."

Miss Becher touched my shoulder. "Oh, my poor child. I've been so worried about your mother as of late. She hasn't been eating well—hasn't been taking care of herself."

"You don't understand," I said. "Mama is alive! She'll be just fine as soon as she warms up. I need to get things ready for her."

Mrs. Myers reached out. "Let me take the babe, Mem, to make sure she hasn't suffered ill from the cold."

It was hard to let loose of her, but I needed to make my preparations for Mama. Still, as Mrs. Myers slipped Lily from my arms, I felt as if a part of me was being wrenched away. "Did your mother say anything to you?" she asked. "Was she sleeping or awake?"

"She'll wake up as soon as she gets into the warm cabin," I said. "She's just chilled from the frost."

I climbed up to the loft and tossed my quilts through the hole to the downstairs floor, then went back down the ladder and gathered the quilts from Mama's bed. I dragged a bench to the hearth and draped the quilts over it to warm them. Some of the women tried to help me, but I told them I wanted to do it myself. I caught two of them whispering and looking at me from across the room with pity in their eyes. "Thank you for your help, but you don't need to stay," I said. "We're going to be just fine, and I can manage alone." I turned the quilts several times to warm them clear through.

Then I went to the cupboard and took out Mama's fine teapot. I felt in my pocket for the packet of tea. It was soaked clear through, but that didn't matter. After all, tea was made by putting it in hot water, so a little cold

water couldn't hurt. I unfolded the paper and dumped
the wad of wet leaves into the pot, then dipped simmer-
ing water from the kettle over it. I'd never paid much
mind to how Mama made tea, but this was close enough.
I put the lid back on the pot, then covered it with a
square of folded wool to keep the warmth in while it
steeped. Already I could smell the fragrant steam from
the spout.

I got out one of Mama's bone china teacups and set it
on the table. I wanted these women to see what a fine
lady Mama had been in Connecticut, to have such a
lovely tea set.

Just then there was a commotion at the door and the
men came in carrying Mama. Before I could stop them,
they laid her on the bed.

"No, over here! She needs to be close to the hearth." I
yanked the quilts off the bench, folding two of them
quickly to make a soft bed.

The men made no effort to move her. "Leave her be,
child," said the one with the beard.

"Please bring her over by the fire," I said. "I'll spoon
sips of tea into her. She loves tea."

The men headed for the door, leaving Mama on the
bed. Miss Becher put her arm around me. "Your mother
was out in the cold all night, Mem. And you know the
cough she's had lately. She must have been too weak. . . ."

I shrugged her arm from my shoulders. "Lily was in

the cold, too, but she's as healthy as ever. Besides, the tea will ease Mama's cough."

I looked at the women who stood around the edges of the room. Not one made a move. Two of them were crying.

Miss Becher grasped my elbow and tried to pull me away from Mama. "You can't help her, Mem."

"Yes, I can!" I wrenched free from her grip and ran to get a quilt. "Here, Mama. Feel how nice and warm this is." I spread it over her, tucked it in around her feet, and pulled it up under her chin. "I have the most wonderful surprise, Mama." I went back to the table and poured the tea. As the amber liquid filled the cup, its aroma spread through the cabin, reminding me of teatime in Connecticut.

My hands trembled as I carried the cup across the room, making it clatter against the saucer. "Look, Mama. I've made tea for you. *Real* tea."

Miss Becher took me firmly by the shoulders and steered me away from the bed. "Mem, you must let your mother go." She turned me around and looked straight into my eyes. And before she said another word, I knew in my heart what I had probably known since I first found Mama in the woods.

This time, she had left us forever.

Seventeen

I felt as if someone had turned a key that locked up my heart. Miss Becher took me over to the bench by the hearth. She had her arm around me and was saying something in a low, soothing voice, but I couldn't make any sense of her words. Then Papa came back from somewhere with Joshua. In all the commotion, I hadn't even noticed they weren't in the cabin.

Poor Joshua didn't understand what had happened to Mama. He got loose from Papa and ran to her. "Mama!" he cried.

Papa managed to scoop Joshua up in his arms just before he got to the bed. "Mama!" Joshua screamed again, leaning down to reach her, stretching out his fingers.

Papa headed for the door, then looked over and saw me. He held out his hand. I ran to Papa, jumping up and wrapping my arms around his neck. He pushed open the door with his elbow and carried us both outside to Mama's garden bench. Some men were sitting there, but they got up and moved away when they saw us coming.

We sat huddled together—Joshua screaming, Papa sobbing, and me with my face buried in Papa's shirt, ashamed that I couldn't shed even one tear for poor Mama.

That whole morning was like a bad dream. Nothing seemed familiar to me. We were surrounded by strangers, and I stayed off to myself so I wouldn't have to talk to anyone. I was sure that everybody knew that I had caused my mother's death. Miss Becher tried to approach me a few times, but I turned away and walked in the opposite direction until she gave up.

I was sitting alone on the garden bench when a wagon rolled in. It was the awful Crowell brothers with a man I guessed to be their father. He was short and stocky with a bushy beard and mustache showing under his battered hat. He pulled the horses to a stop and heaved himself out of the seat. "Fetch your pa for me, girl."

"Yes, sir," I said, glad to have a reason not to talk to Henry and Leonard. They sat slouched in the back of the wagon and didn't seem inclined to speak to me, either. I found Papa with some other men behind the cabin. The women were inside, getting Mama bathed and dressed for burial, and the men stayed outside out of respect.

"Papa, there's a man here to see you."

"Oh?"

"It's those dreadful Crowell boys and their father," I

whispered as we walked around the cabin. "I know them from school."

"If they've come to pay their respects, we accept it, Mem. Doesn't matter what your dealings with them have been in the past."

Papa walked over to Mr. Crowell and extended his hand.

Mr. Crowell took off his hat and ducked his head as he shook hands with Papa. "I'm Jake Crowell. Heard about your wife. I'm sorry."

"Thank you," Papa said, and the two men stood awkwardly, neither knowing what to say next.

Mr. Crowell pointed to the wagon. "You have need of a coffin?"

"Yes," Papa said, "of course." He rubbed his hand across his forehead. "I haven't figured out what to do about that."

Mr. Crowell motioned for the boys to come. They jumped down and slid a pile of wide pine boards out of the wagon bed. "I'd be happy to help you put one together," Mr. Crowell said.

Papa just stared at him.

Mr. Crowell ducked his head again and pretended to be brushing something from the brim of his hat. "Course if you'd rather do it yourself, or you have somebody else doing it for you . . ."

"No! No, I don't. But I . . . it's just that I have . . ." Papa waved his hands in the air helplessly.

Mr. Crowell looked straight ahead, avoiding Papa's eyes. "If you don't like the wood, makes no matter to me. Just say the word and I'll take it away."

"No," Papa said. "It's fine wood, but . . . well, I can't pay you right now. I don't know what I might have to trade."

Mr. Crowell looked Papa right in the eye. "No need to pay me now or later." He coughed and cleared his throat. "I couldn't pay for a coffin when my wife died a few years back, and George Pierce gave me the wood. Helped me build it." Mr. Crowell pushed out his chin, which made him look mean, but I could see that the corners of his eyes were watered up.

Papa shook his hand again. "I'd be honored if you'd help me, Jake. I've never built a coffin before."

"It's a skill you don't want to have a use for," Mr. Crowell said. "Though I've seen enough poor souls go to their reward in recent years to keep a coffin maker occupied full-time." He and Papa and the boys carried the boards out to the shed. Some of the other men joined them, and soon I could hear the sounds of sawing and hammering. In less than an hour, they carried a long pine box out of the shed and into the cabin. It had the terrible shape of all coffins, wider where the shoulders would be and tapered by the head and feet.

More people arrived, a few in wagons, but most on foot. I didn't know there were this many people living close by. I stayed back off the path where I could watch the goings-on but not be seen. Papa came out of the cabin and called to me. He looked worried, and I could tell he was asking the men near the cabin if they'd seen me. Part of me wanted to run to him, but I couldn't move and I couldn't make myself answer him. He headed toward the field, shouting my name.

People kept gathering near the cabin. I recognized some from the search, but many of them I'd never seen before. What good could they do Mama now? How she would have loved visitors when she was alive—when she was still Mama. She would have been so proud to bring out her china teapot and cups. The only one who ever used Mama's good china was hateful old Mrs. Foster. I noticed the old crow hadn't come to Mama's funeral. It was a good thing.

I was startled to hear something brush against the tree next to me. It was Miss Becher. I turned to run, but she caught my arm. "Mem, I know this is awful for you, but you must come and be with your family."

"I can't," I said, but I didn't try to run away from her.

"Your mother was wearing this. The women thought you'd want to have it to remember her by." I turned away, but as she pulled something from her pocket, I caught a glint of gold from the corner of my eye. It was Grandma's locket. Just seeing it made the tears that wouldn't come before spring to my eyes. "It was mine," I said. "I gave it to Mama."

"Then all the more reason for you to have it." Miss

Becher put the locket in my palm and folded my fingers around it. She wiped my tears with her handkerchief, then smoothed back my hair and put a small black veil over my head. "Come," she said, holding out her hand.

"I can't."

"Yes, you can. You must." She took my hand in hers. "We'll go together."

Still I pulled back. "I can't face all those people," I said. "They all know."

"Know what?"

"That I caused Mama's death." The words felt like a knife going into my stomach.

Miss Becher wrapped her arms around me. "Oh, my poor child. You did more for your mother than anyone. Land sakes, you've been caring for her as if she were the child and you the mother. You have no cause to blame yourself for what happened."

I wished I could believe what Miss Becher was saying, but in my heart, I knew that I had let Mama down.

Miss Becher lifted the veil to wipe my new tears, then took the locket from me and fastened it around my neck. "You just keep that foolish notion out of your head and remember that you did your best. That's all any of us can do." She rearranged the veil, and I felt somehow protected by it, as if people couldn't see into my eyes and know the truth. Miss Becher took my hand again. "Now, come with me."

The people who had gathered in front of the house

separated to make a path for us. Papa met us at the door and hugged me. I took a deep breath and went inside with him. Mama's coffin was on the table, surrounded by tansy and rosemary leaves. It made me remember Grandma Nye's funeral, but now, instead of an old woman in the coffin, there was my beautiful mama. The women had dressed her in a white shroud and her freshly washed hair shone in the candlelight, braided the way she had always worn it. I couldn't bear to look. I turned and sobbed into Papa's jacket.

"Your mama's found peace now," Papa said, his voice husky. He led me to a bench, and Ethel Myers brought Joshua over to sit with us while all those strange people filed past Mama's coffin, then came over to speak kindly to us. I wanted to scream, "Where were you all when Mama needed you?" but I held my tongue. How could they have known?

As soon as all the people had paid their respects, Papa led us outside. The sun shone bright in the sky, and it made me angry. I wanted the skies to shed tears for Mama, and instead they were smiling.

It wasn't long before six men came out with Mama's closed coffin on their shoulders and we started the walk to the grave site. Papa had chosen the clearing near the creek where Mama and I had once picked wildflowers. I could still remember her weaving a wreath for my hair.

We had a simple service at the grave—prayers and a few hymns. Joshua got so upset when they started lowering Mama's coffin into the ground, I took his hand and led him back to the cabin. Even from a distance, we could still hear the clods of earth hitting the coffin lid. It was a sound I'd never forget.

Ethel Myers had just carried some water from the creek and looked up as we approached the cabin. "Mem, my daughter Amanda has been caring for Lily today. I want to show you some things about tending to her."

"I can tend to Lily just fine," I said. "I've been doing it since the day she was born."

"I never meant to say you haven't taken good care of the babe," Mrs. Myers said. "You've raised her up right well. But you'll need to be feeding her a new way now, and I'd like Amanda to show you how before the others get back."

Feeding Lily! I'd been so caught up in my own misery, I hadn't given a thought to her. I felt my face go hot with shame. "Has someone been feeding her today?" I asked.

Mrs. Myers pushed open the door, and Amanda was inside, sitting at the table, holding Lily. "Amanda has a babe of her own, and she's nursed Lily along with him. Now that's one way to handle things, if you want Amanda to take Lily until she's weaned."

"No!" I said, running over to take Lily from Amanda's arms. "Mama would want her to stay with us." The thought of having to give up Lily so soon after losing Mama terrified me.

Amanda handed Lily to me and motioned for me to sit

beside her on the bench. "It's all right, Mem. There are ways to feed a babe without nursing her. Look, I've mixed up a gruel." She dipped her finger into a bowl of thin white gruel and coaxed it into Lily's mouth. "Just mind you give her little bits at first until she gets used to it. You can spoon some meat broth into her, too, long as it's not too hot. And she should be able to take some cow's milk." She handed me the bowl and I tried it, glad to have something to do to keep me from thinking of Mama. Lily sucked eagerly at my finger, her eyes wide. "Whoa, Lily!" I said, surprised that I could barely pull my finger away from her. "Let go so I can get some more for you."

Joshua sat next to me and leaned in close to watch. "She likes it. Can I feed her some?"

"Just get some on the end of your finger," I said. "She'll take it."

Joshua tried it and giggled. "It tickles!"

Joshua and I took turns giving Lily fingers of gruel until the bowl was almost empty.

"That's good," Mrs. Myers said. "I'll show you how to make the gruel in a bit. And if you have any questions, our farm is the second one toward Williamson, barely a mile up the post road. You come to me for anything you need, hear? We're all so busy, we don't always notice when we could be of help, but we always have time for neighbors. I would have been here in a minute if I had only known." She shook her head. "But talking about what's over and done with don't help anybody."

We were interrupted by the others coming back from the grave site. Mrs. Myers and the other women busied themselves serving up a meal. I wiped the gruel from Lily's chin and carried her outside. I had just settled into a quiet spot under a tree when Miss Becher came over to sit with me. She looked up at the sky, shading her eyes from the sun. "Looks as if summer might finally be here, now that it's almost time for fall."

"I hope so," I said.

Miss Becher smoothed out her skirt, pressing the creases of the pleats with her fingers. I could tell she had something to say. Finally she looked up. "I just wanted to let you know I'll be boarding with the Myers family now, so I won't be far away."

"You can't stay with us?" I asked.

She shook her head. "I'd like to, but the school board only allows me to stay with families where there's . . ." She worked at her pleats again for a minute, then frowned. "Well, with your mother gone, the school board says it wouldn't be proper for me to stay here."

"Oh," I said, understanding for the first time that many things would be different from now on.

"I want you to continue your studies, Mem."

"I'll be too busy with chores and Lily, Miss Becher. Joshua can go to school, but not me."

"I know you won't be able to come to school, but since I'm living nearby, I'll try to come after school to see you. I can help out with some of your chores, too, when I have the time." Miss Becher leaned over and touched Lily's cheek, then gathered up her skirts and stood. "I'll bring a book and slate for you tomorrow. You could make a fine teacher if you put your mind to it, Mem. You're bright and resourceful. You've learned a great deal about life for one so young."

That made me smile. For a teacher who thought I couldn't read, Miss Becher had a powerful lot of faith in me. I didn't see how I could still dream of being a teacher, but I'd welcome the chance to continue my studies at home.

I sat for a long while after Miss Becher left, watching the people milling around the cabin. I recognized only a few people who had been here at our cabin raising a little more than a year ago. The others had moved on, like the Pierces. Yet these strangers stepped forward as soon as they knew we needed help. Stingy old Mr. Crowell, who wouldn't give firewood to the school, gave Papa enough good milled pine to build Mama's coffin. And a woman who had just met me gave me shoes when she saw me barefoot in the cold.

Papa saw me sitting under the tree and came over. He sighed and put his arm around me, almost waking Lily, who had drifted off to sleep. He didn't speak, and I didn't know what to say, so we sat in an uncomfortable silence. "Your mother would still be alive if it wasn't for me," he said finally.

I looked up at him, startled by what he had said. "No, Papa, it was my fault. I was the one who left her alone."

Papa rubbed his forehead with his free hand. "Your mother never wanted to come here. I almost think she knew it would kill her. But I was too bullheaded to listen to her."

"You thought you were doing what was best for us, Papa. You didn't know what would happen."

"No, I didn't, but when your mother started acting . . . well, when she wasn't herself, I shouldn't have kept people away. Maybe someone could have helped her. The midwife . . . what was her name?"

"Mrs. Pierce," I said, the memory of my broken friendship with Hannah flashing through my mind.

"That's right . . . Rebecca Pierce. She might have known what to do. I just didn't want anyone to know about your mother. I thought it was nobody's business but ours."

"You were ashamed," I blurted, then felt my face go hot as I realized I was talking about myself as much as Papa.

Papa nodded. "I was," he said quietly. I reached over and squeezed his hand.

"Your grandmother might have helped her," Papa continued. "You were right to send her the letter. That reminds me . . ." He reached into his pocket and pulled out a folded piece of paper. "Your mother had this tucked in the bodice of her dress."

"The letter? The letter from Grandma?"

Papa unfolded the paper. "No, it's from your aunt Lydia."

I caught my breath. "Is something wrong with Grandma?"

"I don't think it's too serious," Papa said. "Lydia says your grandmother was ill earlier this summer and doesn't have her strength back enough to travel yet. I'm sure your mother was upset by the news, though."

"I think she was trying to go back to Connecticut to see Grandma, don't you, Papa? And she got confused and lost." Though it didn't help Mama now, I felt better knowing what she might have been thinking when she left the cabin.

Papa nodded. "That could be. I should have taken her back before it was too late." He leaned against the tree. "Maybe that's where we all should be going," he said after another long silence.

"Back to Connecticut?" I had never dared to hope that we'd go back home, although I'd secretly dreamed many times what it would be like to have our whole family together again.

"The letter said your uncle Henry broke his leg and had to hire someone to do field work," Papa said. "Maybe I could work for him instead. And you have the new babe to care for. Your aunt Lydia would give you a hand with her. Your aunt Sally, too."

I held my breath, afraid that I might say something that would cause Papa to change his mind.

"Of course, we can't be leaving right away," Papa continued. "First I'll have to sell the farm. But George Pierce and some others have sold their land. There's no reason I can't do the same. It won't be the way it was before, Mem. I'm not sure we can get much for our land. And we probably won't have our own place for a while in Connecticut. We'll be living with Henry and Lydia and their family. We'll all be sleeping in their spare room, I'd guess."

"That's fine, Papa. I don't mind." Aunt Lydia and Uncle Henry had bought Grandma and Grandpa's farmstead when they moved into town. I loved the big old house and barns. What difference would it make if our family was packed into one room? It couldn't be any worse than being crowded into a one-room cabin.

All that time waiting for Grandma to come, and now we were going back to her instead of the other way around. It broke my heart that Mama couldn't return to the home she loved. I wished that I could have saved her or that she might have found the strength to save herself. I knew I had to be strong for Joshua and Lily, and I'd tell them stories about Mama so they'd have a memory of her. I needed to remember her for myself, too, the way she used to be when she was still Mama.

Papa stood and looked toward the cornfield. I could tell he was picturing in his mind what this farm might have become. I knew how hard it must be for him to give up and go back home. Poor Papa had thought farming would be easier in the Genesee Country, but the terrible weather had defeated him.

As I watched Papa walk to the cabin, I pulled the locket out from under my dress and held it by the chain so that it swung back and forth in the sunshine. Lily watched it, gurgling with joy. I freed her from her swaddling cloths so she could wave her arms and kick her feet.

Though Mama's life had ended, Lily's was just beginning. With the help of Grandma and my aunts, I knew I could raise her to be strong so that no matter what happened, she'd always know how to take care of herself.

I could feel the dreadful weight begin to lift from my shoulders. We were going back to our family. After all that had happened here in the wilderness, we were going home.

Author's Note

Frozen Summer was intended to be a single book, not part of a trilogy. Reading news stories about people who thought the world would end in the year 2000, I decided to write a "millennium book." First I tried to find information about the turning of the last millennium, but that period in history didn't fire my imagination. I let go of the millennium theme and started searching for other events in history that might have convinced some people that the world was ending. When I read accounts of 1816, the year without a summer, I knew I had found my subject. I decided to set the book where I live in New York State, which was then called "the Genesee Country," and I began researching in earnest.

I wanted the story to revolve around a young girl whose family had recently moved into the area, since this would make them more vulnerable to a crop failure.

After reading about the difficult life of women in the early settlements, I also knew that the girl's mother would go mad and possibly die in the bleak conditions of the wilderness. I chose the title, *Frozen Summer,* to represent not only the weather conditions but also the chilling effect of Mem's relationship with her mother as Aurelia drifts away from her. When I got into the book, I realized the story should start earlier to show the family back in their Connecticut home. Then when I delved into the research for the journey, I felt that was a story in itself, and I wrote *Journey to Nowhere*. I've written *Frozen Summer* to stand alone, but the reader will have a richer experience by meeting the family first in *Journey to Nowhere*.

Though the characters in the book never find out what caused their disastrous summer, the reader should know the facts. In April 1815, Tambora, a huge volcano, erupted in the southern Indonesian islands. It wiped out all but twenty-six of the twelve thousand people living on Sumbawa Island and spewed a hundred times more ash into the atmosphere than Mount Vesuvius in A.D. 79 or Mount Saint Helens in 1980. But the island residents weren't the only ones to feel the effects of Tambora. The volcanic dust was carried through the high stratosphere and reduced the sunlight enough to cause the year that settlers later referred to as "Eighteen Hundred and Froze to Death." After an unusually cold spring, snows in June and killing frosts in the other summer months were felt throughout northern New England and New York.

Most people probably hadn't heard about the eruption of Tambora, and even those who had wouldn't be likely to make the connection to something that had happened a year before and so far away. If Benjamin Franklin had still been alive, he might have cleared up the mystery. He had suspected that the cold winter of 1783–1784 might have been caused by volcanoes. Though most weren't familiar with Franklin's theory, they all knew about his invention of the lightning rods that adorned many barns in the area. Since the belief at the time was that the earth was heated by fluid electricity running through the ground, some blamed the lightning rods for interrupting the flow of electricity and causing the cold weather. Others thought the appearance of sunspots had caused the weather disturbance. In reading both diaries and newspapers from the period, I was surprised that people wrote about viewing these sunspots with the naked eye. Apparently the haze in the atmosphere that summer allowed people to look directly at the sun when it was rising or setting.

It was fascinating to read diaries written by Genesee Country residents from the summer of 1816 since many people noted the temperatures and weather for each day. Almost all of them mentioned the snow on June 6, but the frosts in late June and early July seemed to be spotty, killing the crops in one area while sparing another. It is said that the town of Egypt, New York, got its name from the fact that its fields were spared from the frosts while the crops in the surrounding towns were destroyed.

Since there was no ready explanation for the weather, some felt that God was angry with them. A newspaper article in the July 2, 1816, *Ontario Respository* warned that the "Almighty [will] visit us with the most dreadful scourge of nations—famine!" Throughout the year, itinerant preachers rode around their circuits, holding church services in private homes. But it was the camp meetings, usually conducted by Baptists and Methodists, that appealed to the emotions and stirred up religious fervor. The description of the camp meeting ground outside of Lyons, New York, came from a journal kept by De Witt Clinton. I found evidence of an increase in spiritual interest in 1816–1817, and Lyons was listed as one of the sites for the many revivals.

Up until the Great Awakening, a series of religious revivals among Protestants, in the mid–eighteenth century, mental illness was thought to have supernatural causes. It was felt that the devil could cause madness in both sinners and holy men. Ministers were called to perform days of fasting and prayer with the afflicted person and his family to cure the condition. But the Great Awakening gave more responsibility to the individual for his own salvation. Madness was now thought to be under a person's own control and therefore a matter of shame.

Life was difficult for women in the nineteenth century even under the best of conditions, so they counted on the support of their friends and female relatives in times of crisis. A woman about to give birth would gather her women around her, and they were as important as the midwife who actually helped with the delivery. The women who moved from the close-knit communities of New England into the seclusion of a cabin in the Genesee Country were often cut off from that support. In my author's notes for *Journey to Nowhere*, I mentioned being led to the diary of Candace Beach by Lynne Belluscio, director of the Leroy Historical Society. Candace Beach became a teacher in Leroy, New York, hired to start in April and teach for six months. This is a different school schedule from what I have seen in other books, but I chose to use the primary source for my information.

Most of the women's diaries I have read reveal little about the women's inner thoughts but simply list the day's activities. Candace Beach was more open about her feelings with phrases such as "My spirits are very low. . . . I feel quite discouraged. . . . I am homesick indeed this morning. . . . Though the face wears a smile of contentment yet it often conceals a sickening heart." She also mentions several deaths in the town and, although in apparent good health, comments, "I know not whether I shall live to see another year." Candace Beach lived in a much more settled community than Aurelia Nye and was able to see her relatives every week or so. It seemed to me that Aurelia, miles away from her family and isolated from neighbors, would have few resources to keep her from sinking into the depths of despair.

In spite of the harsh summer of 1816, it seems remarkable that so many of the settlers had enough resilience to keep going. Prodded into action by the cold summer, thousands piled into their wagons and headed even farther west. The population of Indiana increased by forty-two thousand in 1816. So the summer that some believed to foretell the end of the world led to the beginning of a better life for those who had the courage to take the leap into the new frontier.